SCARLET SUN

ISABEL HANSEN

I ALWAYS THOUGHT the summer after my first year of university would be magical. After all, I was returning home after eight months of living in residence — I would get to spend time with my family again, I could eat actually good food instead of the junk they served in the cafeteria, I wouldn't have to share a bathroom with thirty other girls, and, most of all, I would have my own room.

I definitely over-idealized that idea in my mind.

My family was annoying me to no end, I apparently remembered my parents' cooking wrong because it tasted barely better than what I had in the cafeteria at school, sharing a bathroom with my little sister was somehow worse than sharing it with thirty other college girls, and though having my own room was nice, it was also a total mess (and I would never admit this, but I missed my roommate, Elyssa).

I kicked my now empty duffel bag across the room and ran my hands through my hair. I had finally finished unpacking after coming home, but although my clothes were nearly put away, the rest of my room was still in disarray.

"I thought I was supposed to be relaxing after exams," I muttered to myself as I turned to clean up my desk. I'd meant to clean my room before leaving for school so I wouldn't have to deal with it when I came back, but of course, my laziness had won out, and I'd left the problem for my future self. Now cursing my past self for making that decision, I began the tedious task of sorting through the massive piles of paper on my desk. I pulled my small recycling bin over to beside the desk and began throwing out everything that I no longer needed.

There was a small knock on the door.

"Come in!" I called. I turned to see who was there. In the doorway was my eight-year-old sister, Jean. I smiled. Although we had a twelve-year age difference, I always enjoyed spending time with my sister. "Hey Jeanie. What's up?"

"What are you doing?" Jean asked, walking into the room.

"I'm decluttering my room. Want to help?"

Jean shrugged. "Sure."

"Can you sort through the papers and tell me if any of them don't look like they came from a school note-book?" I asked, pointing to a stack of papers on the main part of the desk. Most of them were old high school notes, but I worried about throwing them out without at least confirming that there wasn't anything important in the pile.

"Okay!" Jean said, bouncing on her toes.

"Thank you," I said, ruffling her hair briefly.

I went back to sorting through my own pile, but it

was only thirty seconds later that I was interrupted by Jean going, "Hey what's this?"

I looked over as Jean tugged a small paper out of the middle of the pile, almost toppling the whole thing over. She held the page triumphantly. Unlike the other standard notebook pages, it was light pink and had drawings of flowers at the top.

"It looks like it's from my old diary," I muttered. I gently took the paper out of Jean's hands and looked it over. At the top of the page, it said, 20 THINGS I WANT TO DO BEFORE I'M 20. Underneath was a list:

1. *Go skinny dipping*
2. *Get a tattoo*
3. *Go on a road trip*
4. *Go camping in Algonquin*
5. *Watch the sunrise*
6. *Hike a mountain*
7. *Learn how to drive*
8. *Dance in the rain*
9. *Conquer a fear*
10. *Swim in the ocean*
11. *Fall in love — real love*
12. *Dye my hair*
13. *Read 100 books in one year*
14. *Learn a second language*
15. *Run a 10K*
16. *Learn how to play an instrument*
17. *Graduate high school*
18. *Donate blood*

19. Be out and proud
20. Make a new list: 30 things to do before 30

Jean looked at me with wide, curious eyes.

"Well?" She prompted when I didn't say anything. She put her fists on her hips and tapped her foot. "What is it?"

"It's nothing," I said. I put the paper on the top shelf of my desk, much higher than she could reach, and turned back to the task at hand. "Just some stupid list I wrote in high school."

Jean crossed her arms and looked up at the paper that was out of her reach with a large sigh. I rolled my eyes. She really needed to learn that she was not entitled to everything just because she wanted it.

"Are you going to help me, or just stand there pouting?" I asked. Jean sighed quite loudly again, but then grabbed another small pile of papers to sort through. We worked in silence for a couple of minutes before Jean couldn't hold in her questions anymore.

"What kind of list was it?" She asked.

I shrugged, not looking up from the papers in my hands. "Just a list."

"Right, but what kind of list?"

Recognizing that Jean would not give up until she got what she considered a satisfactory answer, I said, "It's a list of things I wanted to do by this summer."

Jean frowned. "Why this summer?"

"Because I turn twenty years old this summer," I said. I threw a stack of old high school tests in the recycling bin beside me. "There were some things I wanted to do before my twentieth birthday."

Jean nodded solemnly. "How many have you completed?"

"I don't know," I said.

"All of them?"

"Definitely not."

"But some of them?"

"Yeah, I think so."

Jean huffed, getting tired of my short answers. "Are you going to finish them?"

"I don't know," I said.

Jean huffed again. "I'm going downstairs."

"Okay."

Jean faltered, as though she expected I to stop her. I assumed she was only pretending to want to leave in the hopes that I would ask her to stay. Then, she would use wanting to know more about the list as leverage. But I could see straight through her.

"I'm really leaving," Jean said. She took a step closer to the door. I glanced up.

"Okay, I'll see you later."

Jean frowned, but she did walk out. I shut the door behind her, then tried to get back to work. But within a couple of minutes, I found myself distracted again. What was on that list? I hadn't looked it over very carefully before. How many of the items had I completed? Which ones were left? Was it possible for me to finish it before my birthday in two months?

I grabbed the list from the shelf and looked it over. Skinny dipping? I had never done that. Get a tattoo? I already had two. I glanced over the rest of the list. I wagered that I'd done about half of the items on the list. Whether or not I wanted to do the rest was a toss-up. Some of them were easy: dance in the rain, watch the sunrise, dye my hair. But some of them would be much harder, whether it be from an organizational standpoint or an emotional one: go on a road trip, conquer a fear, fall in love. I supposed if I really dedicated some time to it, I might be able to finish them, but it would definitely take a lot of effort.

I grabbed my phone and sent a picture of the list to my best friends group chat with the text, *think I can manage it?* It was a resounding yes from Bree and Kiara, ever the optimists, while Elyssa seemed unsure, and Harlee said there was absolutely no way. Although I knew Harlee was probably joking, hearing someone tell me I couldn't do it made me want to try even more.

If there was one thing I enjoyed in life, it was proving people wrong.

ON FRIDAY AFTERNOON, I drove the two hours from my house to Kiara's house in another town. Part of the fun, if you could call it that, of making friends at university was that we all lived in different towns. Of everyone I met, none were from the same town as me — although I was admittedly from a pretty small place, so that was not unexpected. But none of my friends were even from the same town as each other, save for Kiara and Harlee who had been best friends for years and had chosen to go to university together. My friends lived all over the province, all over the country in fact, and that made it incredibly inconvenient to visit them.

I tapped my hands against the steering wheel to the beat of the music as I drove along. Whenever my favourite songs came on, which were few and far between, mind you, I sang along to them. I enjoyed singing along to music when I drove, but I hated the idea of somebody seeing me. While for the most part, I tried to ignore what other thought of me, I could never shake the feeling of how stupid I must look when I was doing so.

It was the first time I was ever visiting Kiara's house. I had visited the town, East Port, only once before, for Harlee's New Year's Eve party. I hadn't had time nor reason to go to Kiara's house on that day. As such, I had no idea that Kiara's house was quite so far. My GPS led me down a long winding road that, if I hadn't had a map right in front of me telling me otherwise, I would have said leads straight out of town. Even though I was certain I'd put the address in right and I trusted that Kiara had given me the right address, I kept checking the GPS every minute or two, as if it was going to suddenly change and tell me I was going the wrong way. The longer I drove down this empty road, the more uneasy I felt. My grip on the steering wheel was so tight that the skin over my knuckles had gone completely white. When a squirrel ran in front of my car, I nearly screamed. I slammed on the brakes so hard that my body slammed forward, the seat belt digging into my neck. I had to take a couple of moments to collect myself.

Maybe I shouldn't have watched that horror movie last night.

I'm not usually a fan of horror movies, but Elyssa kept raving about it to me and I had to see what the fuss was about. Personally, I don't think it was all that good, but I didn't tell her that.

I also didn't tell her that I screamed more than once while watching it. I have a reputation to maintain, after all.

I glanced at my GPS again. It said I was finally approaching my destination, but when I looked ahead, all I saw was open road. I frowned and turned down my music, as if that would help me find my way at all. I heard my dad's voice in my head: *I can't see when you play your music that loud! Turn it down.* I never understood him saying that until I learned to drive myself and had the same issue.

Finally, the GPS told me to turn right at the next road. It appeared out of nowhere, but once I turned on it, I breathed a sigh of relief as I saw a line of houses. For some reason, this seemed to be a small suburban neighbourhood that was greatly disconnected from the rest of the town. Kiara's house was only one block in. I turned into the driveway and parked in front of the closed garage doors, just like she told me to. By the time I climbed out of the car, Kiara and Harlee were walking out the front door.

"April!" Kiara called. She ran down the front steps, and more or less tackled me in a hug, knocking the breath out of me. If you've ever gotten hugged by a girl who played hockey in high school, you'll understand the feeling. She pulled back again, though she kept her hands planted firmly on my upper arms, and smiled widely. "How are you? I've missed you so much!"

"I'm good, Kiara," I said. "I've missed you too. But it has only been two weeks."

"Two weeks is way too long!" Kiara said. She glanced back at Harlee, who was standing a few feet behind her, with an amused look on her face. "Isn't it Harlee?"

Harlee nodded ever-so-slightly. I think, like me, she thought that two weeks was hardly anything, but she didn't want to disagree with Kiara.

"We're happy you could visit so soon," she said.

To my surprise, I found that they both looked a bit different than they had when I'd seen them last. Harlee was beautiful as ever; her long and dark brown hair was shiny and sleek, her makeup was perfectly done (her eyeliner was sharp enough to cut somebody with — I'd never understood how she did it), and she had clearly just gotten a manicure, as she had light pink acrylics on her hands. It was a far cry from how she'd looked throughout exam season, where she'd barely bothered to get ready every morning before she started to study.

Kiara, on the other hand, had made a much more drastic change.

"You cut your hair!" I exclaimed. I ran my fingers through the ends of her strawberry blonde hair, which now just reached her chin in a chic bob. For as long as I'd known her, and I believe for most of her life actually, Kiara had kept her hair long. Like, extremely long. By the time she had started university, it was well past her waist.

"I did," she said. She ran a hand through it, shifting it from a right part to a left one. "Do you like it?"

"It looks awesome!" I said. "It really suits you."

She beamed. "Thank you!"

"Do you need help carrying your stuff in?" Harlee asked. She held a hand up to block the sun from her eyes.

"It's fine, I don't have a lot." I popped open my trunk and grabbed the small duffel bag I'd brought for the trip. My keys and phone were already in my hands, so I had everything I might need for the weekend. "Actually, can one of you close the trunk for me?"

"Yeah, I've got it," Kiara said.

"Thanks." I frowned and looked around. At first, I

had assumed that Bree was busy doing something in the house and that was why she hadn't come to greet me outside, but I didn't see her car anywhere around. "Is Bree not here yet?"

"No, she hit traffic on the way here," Kiara said. The trunk slammed closed. "She should arrive soon though."

"Okay," I said. Unfortunately, Elyssa wasn't able to come for just the weekend since she lived so far away from us.

"Come on, I'll show you around," Kiara said. She grabbed my hand and pulled me forward. The house was big and very open concept. As soon as we stepped inside, I could see most of the main floor, except for the section that was blocked by the stairs. The house was pretty modern, with dark hardwood floors, leather furniture, and sleek black appliances. Although there were sheer blinds covering all the windows, the house was full of natural light. "My bedroom is upstairs, but we were thinking of sleeping in the basement instead since it's a lot bigger. Are you okay with that?"

Honestly, I was a little wary of going down to the basement after watching that horror movie but I didn't want to mess up her plans, so I said, "Yeah, that's fine."

"Great!" Kiara said. She continued to pull me forward. "So obviously this is the main floor. As you can see, the dining room is here, the kitchen is up ahead, and the living room is across from it. The sliding glass doors over there lead out to the backyard, but there's also a door from the basement that we'll probably use more often."

She opened the door to the basement and turned on the light. As we walked down the white stairs, I was relieved to see that the basement was also very open concept and bright, unlike the one in the horror movie. We walked to the far end, where there were three couches forming a semi-circle around a TV that was mounted on the wall above the fireplace.

"This is where we're going to sleep," Kiara explained. "We can either sleep on the couches, or we can use the air mattresses. We just have to get them out of the garage and set them up."

"And hope that they actually work this time," Harlee said with a small grin. "I seem to remember the last time we used those air mattresses, they deflated every twenty minutes."

"Only one of them did!" Kiara defended. "But you're right, the couches would probably be better. We've also got some futon cushions that we can put on the floor."

"All this is to say, we have options," Harlee said. She clapped her hands together. "Can we go to the hot tub now?"

Kiara rolled her eyes. "Sorry about her, she's been asking to go to the hot tub since she got here."

"The fact that you have a hot tub is the only reason I have remained friends with you for so long." She said it in a serious voice, but when I glanced over at her, I could see the humour in her eyes.

"And just for that, you don't get to use the hot tub," Kiara said.

"Hey!"

"Is there somewhere I can get changed?" I asked. I gestured uselessly at my clothes. "I'm not really dressed for going swimming."

"Oh yeah, of course!" Kiara said. She pointed at a

bathroom down the hall. "You can get changed in there if you want."

"Thanks." I grabbed a swimsuit and beach dress from my bag and went down the hall. Although Kiara, Harlee and Elyssa were all more than comfortable changing in front of each other, I generally preferred some privacy.

In the bathroom, I quickly got changed, then pulled my light brown hair out of the ponytail I had been wearing it in while I was driving. I smoothed down my locks as best I could, although it still looked like a mess. I sighed and stared at myself in the mirror. Whatever, I was about to go swimming — what did it matter what my hair looked like? Leaving it as it was, I walked back down the hall.

Kiara and Harlee were standing by the door and each scrolling on their phone, but they perked up when I walked back. I dumped my driving clothes back in my bag, grabbed my sunglasses, and slipped on my flip-flops.

"Let's go," I said.

The large pool took up a good portion of the back-yard. Beside it were a line of lawn chairs, set up perfectly in the sun. Closer to the house, and under the shade of the overhang, was the hot tub. Kiara and Harlee immediately headed there, but I hung back.

"You okay?" Kiara asked when she noticed.

"Yeah, I think I would just rather tan for a bit," I said.

"Here, I'll move one of the chairs closer to the hot tub for you," she said. Kiara was much physically stronger than me, so I stood by patiently as she picked up one of the chairs with ease and moved it closer, while still leaving it in the sun. "Is that good?"

"It's great," I said. "Thanks."

I kicked off my shoes and sat down. I was just settling in when I heard the telltale sound of Bree's truck. Well, it was really her older sister's truck but Bree used it more than her, so it was like it was hers. I groaned as I stood up again. We walked around the side of the house to meet her in the driveway.

"Hey guys!" Bree said, waving at us wildly. Just as she did with me, Kiara ran up to hug her, while Harlee and I hung back for the time being. Bree hugged Kiara back just as enthusiastically, then began fawning over her new haircut.

"My haircut?" Kiara said. "What about yours? It looks fantastic!"

"I didn't get a haircut," Bree laughed. Kiara rolled her eyes.

"I meant your extensions, Bree," she said, shoving her shoulders. With them standing next to each other like that, it looked like they had switched hairstyles. Where Kiara had gone from long hair to a bob, Bree had gone from shoulder-length hair to mid-back length hair. It was dirty blonde and naturally straight, though she had curled it that day. She'd begun growing out her hair in the middle of high school, when she officially came out as trans, but it was a long process to grow it out from how short it had been before, and I knew she had always wanted really long hair.

"It does look very good, Bree," I said. "When did you get it done?"

"Just a couple of days ago," she said with a grin. "It was a present from my parents. So what are we doing today?"

"Well, we were thinking of just sitting in the hot tub for a little while," Kiara said, gesturing to the fact that we were all in beach wear, "then this afternoon, maybe going into town. I know Harlee wanted to go to the bookstore this weekend."

"I just got my final pay check from my job at school and now I want to go spend it," Harlee said. We all laughed, full well knowing that we did the same whenever we got our pay checks.

"That sounds like fun," Bree said. "I just need to change into my swimsuit."

"Oh yeah, no problem," Kiara said. "I'll show you around inside. Harlee and April, you guys can go back to the yard. We'll meet you there in a minute."

"Okay," Harlee said.

When we got back there, Harlee immediately slipped into the hot tub, but I took up my seat in the sun again.

"It's warmer than I expected," I said. I wasn't sure why I said it exactly. I had always thought that making small talk was worse than just not talking at all, and it wasn't like Harlee and I didn't have any other things to talk about. The words just slipped out before I had time to think it over or stop them, and it would be weird if I tried to take them back.

"A bit strange for May," Harlee agreed. She shrugged. "But you never know what the weather will be like around here."

I hummed in agreement, then wracked my brain for anything else to say. I hadn't spoken to anyone outside my family since getting home from university, and it had apparently had an effect on my social skills.

"So what books are you planning to buy when we go into town?" I asked.

"I'm not sure yet. I've got a pretty long list of books I want, but honestly, half the time when I go into a bookstore, I buy a ton of books that I've never even heard of."

"Thereby making your list even longer."

"Exactly." She grabbed a pack of gum from her bag and popped a piece in her mouth. She held up the packet so I could see it. "Want one?"

"Sure." I moved from my seat by the pool to be sitting next to the hot tub, though I didn't climb it. I still found the afternoon air too warm to warrant getting in the hot tub. I wasn't sure how Harlee was managing it. "What flavour is it?"

She flipped the packet over so she could read the name.

"Extreme mint," she read out. "Whatever that means."

It did seem rather ambiguous, but I just shrugged. The patio door opened, and Kiara and Bree walked out, now both dressed in bathing suits. Kiara also had some towels under her arm. It was a good forethought that hadn't even occurred to me.

"Either of you want gum?" Harlee asked. Kiara shook her head, but Bree held out her hand. Harlee popped out a piece for her, before putting the pack back in her bag.

Bree came and sat next to me, then bumped her shoulder against mine.

"Hey, we didn't really get to talk earlier," she said. "How's it going?"

I just shrugged in response. When she continued to stare at me, I cracked and said, "I'm okay."

"You like being home again?" She asked curiously. To be honest, I didn't hate it as much as I thought I would, but it still wasn't my favourite experience. I knew the answer she was looking for, so I just snorted and shook my head. She nodded and squinted up at the sky. Her long hair fell back. "Yeah, me neither."

"I thought you liked spending time with your family."

"I do. But I miss being with you guys more than I like being with them."

Normally Bree didn't say stuff like that. Harlee was the one who spoke in a way that made you stop and think. It made sense, given that she was studying English Literature. So when Bree said that, I had to take a moment to consider it.

"I wouldn't have expected you to compare the experiences," I said finally. Because that was also what Bree was like. She had an optimistic view of the world, and never liked to compare the present to the past, or long for what once was.

She grinned slightly, but still didn't look at me. "I guess you guys are slowly changing me."

"The best friends do," Harlee said with a wink. I laughed hollowly along with them, but there was a small ache in my heart at Bree's words. I didn't want to change her. I wasn't trying to change her. Bree was perfect just as she was, and I would never want to do anything to compromise that.

The conversation turned, but I didn't follow it after that point. I grabbed my phone and opened up my messages. I had a couple of texts from people that I glanced at but didn't bother responding to. I would get to them later. I was pretty sure that most of my family and friends had learned to expect my responses to any non-urgent texts to come in at midnight or later, since I liked to catch up on my messages before I went to bed.

"Isn't that right, April?" Kiara asked. I looked up in surprise. All three of them were looking at me.

"Sorry, I wasn't listening," I said, slipping my phone back into my bag.

"It's fine. I was just complaining about our history professor from last semester," Kiara said.

"Enough talk about school!" Bree said. "I don't want to think about that until September."

"What do you want to talk about, then?" Kiara asked.

Bree shrugged. "Your house is awesome. How long do you have it to yourself?"

"Just the weekend," Kiara said. "My parents will be back Monday evening. Oh, by the way, does anyone want a Palm Bay? I have a bunch in the fridge."

"You want to day drink?" Bree asked with an amused smile.

"Hey, we're on vacation!" Kiara defended. She hopped out of the water. "I'm assuming you all want one. I'll be right back."

Harlee and Bree laughed as she walked away.

"I love summer break," Bree said.

$*$ 3 $*$

We decided to go to the bookstore the next afternoon instead. When we got there, we all split up to look in the sections that we were most interested in. I stuck with Harlee as we made our way to the classics book section. Harlee had the most extensive library of classic books I had ever seen and was always looking to add to the collection. I, on the other hand, had a list of books that I wanted to read, and a good number of them were classics.

"Have you read any Jane Austen?" Harlee asked.

"No," I said. She grabbed three books off the shelf and put them in my hands.

"*Pride and Prejudice* is the obvious one," she said. "But you should also read *Sense and Sensibility* and *Emma*."

"Okay," I said. I glanced at the books in my hand. I was trying to avoid buying too many books, so I didn't want her to pile on any more suggestions. "I think I'm going to get some coffee now."

Harlee nodded. I walked towards the Starbucks that

was tucked into the back corner of the shop. There was no line so I went straight up to order my drink. As I waited for the cashier to write my name on the cup and hand me my change, I looked around and caught sight of Bree standing at the counter where the drinks came out. I hadn't noticed her there before. She was talking to a guy who looked about our age. I narrowed my eyes. The guy seemed to be speaking at her while she was visibly uncomfortable. She had a fake smile plastered on her as she nodded along to what the guy was saying but her eyes were flitting around the room. She and I made eye contact. Her expression screamed *help me!* The cashier gave me my change, and I quickly pocketed it before walking over to the counter where Bree was standing.

"Hey, Bree!" I said. All my books were in my left arm, so I looped my right arm in hers. "How's it going?"

"Um, we're kind of in the middle of a conversation," the guy interrupted. I resisted the urge to roll my eyes.

"And now you're not," I said. When he still didn't walk away, I waved with my fingers and said in a sweet voice, "Bye."

He frowned. He looked at each of us in turn a couple of times with a perplexed look on his face, then, without a word, turned around and walked away.

"Thank you," Bree whispered. She squeezed my hand.

"You didn't look very happy to be talking to him," I said.

"He was going on and on about his fraternity," Bree said. "I could barely get a word in edgewise. Just had to smile and nod."

"Did he think he was impressing you?" I looked over the front of the store, where the guy was now standing with his friends. I wasn't surprised he was a frat dude; he was dressed in gym shorts, a T-shirt, and flip flops.

"I guess so," Bree said.

"You need to learn how to say no to people," I said. Bree was a people-pleaser, and she was almost incapable of saying no to anyone, even if they were being awful to her.

"I know," she sighed.

"Nitro cold brew for April!" The barista called out, sliding the cup across the counter.

"Thank you," I said. I grabbed the drink and we walked back towards the bookshelves. We stopped in the young adult section and I ran my eyes over the book spines.

"I just hate hurting people's feelings," Bree said suddenly. I knew she was still thinking of the boy.

"Even if they're being a dick?"

"Even then," Bree confirmed.

I shook my head. I was still of the mind that she needed to learn to say no to people more than she did, but if I was being entirely honest, I liked how pure her heart was.

"That's what I love about you," I said.

She leaned her head against my shoulder. "I know."

4

"How old did you say you were when you wrote this list, April?" Harlee asked. The four of us were laying on the floor in Kiara's basement. It was late in the evening and we had been watching a movie, which continued to drone on in the background, but everyone's attention had been quickly shifted when Kiara asked to see my bucket list.

"I think I was fourteen," I said. I was a little self-conscious about some of the things that I had added to the list so I added, "Hence why some of the items are pretty stupid."

"I don't think any of them are stupid," Bree said.

"Dance in the rain?" I said. "Learn how to play an instrument? Watch a sunrise?"

"All great goals," Bree maintained. She cleared her throat. "Speaking of which, I think we should have an adventure before we all start working this summer and get too busy to see each other."

"That sounds fun," Kiara said. "What kind of adventure were you thinking?"

"I don't know." Contrary to her words, I got the sense that she had something in mind. "I guess I've always wanted to go on a road trip. And it's on April's list so that would work well."

"A road trip?" Kiara asked. "But where would we go?"

Bree shrugged. "Anywhere. That's the fun of it."

"We could go to Algonquin," I suggested. I pointed to the fourth item on the list. "See? Camping in Algonquin. I've been meaning to do it for ages but I've never gotten around to it."

It was less that I had never gotten around to it, and more that I'd never had anyone interested in coming with me but I didn't add that part.

"How far is that?" Harlee asked.

"Depends where we're leaving from," I said. Given how far apart we lived, the point of origin made a fairly big difference.

"Okay, so for sake of argument, let's say we leave from here," Harlee said. She pulled out her phone and looked it up on maps. "Assuming we don't want to cross the border for part of the drive—"

I cringed at the thought. I had only ever had bad experiences when visiting the United States.

"Why would we want to do that?" I asked.

"I don't know, it's supposedly like thirty minutes faster. Anyway, assuming we want to be in Canada the whole time, it would take just over 21 hours."

Bree raised her eyebrows. "21 hours? That's not terrible."

"It's not great either," I said.

"Only three days if we drive for seven hours every day," Harlee said. "Or five days if we drive for just over four hours. Or—"

"Yeah, we get the picture," I said. In the time that I'd known Harlee, I had learned that she would ramble for hours if she wasn't interrupted. "But remember, it's only 21 hours there. We then have to drive all the way back again too."

"Do you want to go camping in Algonquin or not, April?" Kiara asked. I sighed and looked at the list. This would probably be my only chance to go to Algonquin before my birthday. And how bad could a road trip with friends be?

"When do you want to leave?" I asked.

"I need to be back in five weeks to start my summer job," Harlee said.

"Oh, where are you working?" Bree asked.

"A bookstore." She twirled a pencil in her hands. "It should be fun, I think."

"You'll be able to buy all the books you want," Kiara said. Harlee grinned. I was pretty sure that had been part of her decision to apply for the job.

"I think we can do the trip in three weeks," I said. Really, I thought we could probably do it in two weeks, but it was better to give ourselves extra time. "So maybe we leave next week and that gives us enough time to make sure we're all back in time for our jobs."

"My parents aren't going to be very happy with me packing up and leaving without any warning," Kiara said. "Especially since I just got home for the summer."

"We'll only be gone for a couple of weeks," Bree said. "You really think they'll be that angry?"

"Unfortunately yes," she said. She bit her lip and stared at the ground for a moment in thought. "Oh well, they can't get angry if they don't know about it, right?"

Bree's eyes widened in shock. "What?"

"How exactly are you going to keep it from them, Kiara?" Harlee asked.

"Simple. I'll stay at your house the night before we leave—"

"You will?" Harlee asked with raised eyebrows. I tried to bite back my grin. I knew she was trying to suggest that Kiara would not be staying at her house without invitation but I was certain that when push came to shove, Harlee wouldn't say no and Kiara very well knew it.

"Don't interrupt," Kiara said dismissively. "Anyway, that means that they won't be suspicious about me leaving with my bag and stuff. And then—"

"You'll disappear for three weeks without a word?" I asked in a flat voice.

Kiara rolled her eyes. "Will you guys let me finish? What I was going to say was that I will text them that I am going on a road trip once we're already a couple of hours out of town."

"Won't they be angry?" Bree asked.

"Well, yeah, at first, but they'll have three weeks to calm down before I get back."

"Okay, no offence, Kiara," Harlee said, "but that is the most stupid plan you have ever come up with."

"Well, it's happening," she said stubbornly. "And what does it matter to you, anyway?"

"You mean, besides the fact that you're now apparently staying at my house next week?"

"Only for one night! I'm letting you stay here for the whole weekend!"

"Letting me? You begged me to stay because you were scared of staying home alone."

I grinned as their little argument continued. Although they were best friends, the two of them often butted heads and had small arguments like this. They were never serious and they got over them quickly, so I had no problem with just sitting back and enjoying the show. I glanced at Bree. She was watching them carefully, and slowly eating popcorn. Apparently, she felt the same way then.

"Look, maybe we should get back to planning this," Kiara said. "We leave next week and we'll leave ourselves three weeks to go. Besides Algonquin, is there anywhere anyone wants to go?"

She looked around but none of us said anything.

"How much longer would it be to go to Toronto?" Bree asked finally.

"Probably about three or four hours," Harlee said. "Both ways, of course."

"And it would mean having to either choke up the money for a hotel in Toronto or driving into the city and out in one day," Kiara said. Bree frowned.

"Yeah, that's not worth it," she said.

"We could make it work if you really wanted to," I said. I didn't say it because I knew they would all tell me I didn't need to worry about it, but I felt bad that, thus far, the trip was entirely centred on me and what I wanted to do. I didn't want Bree, or any of them, to feel like they were missing out on something they wanted to do to accommodate my wishes.

Bree brushed off my concern. "No, I don't really care. I was just thinking if we were driving to Ontario anyway, we might as well go if it's convenient."

"Have you ever been?" Harlee asked.

Bree nodded. "My grade eight class field trip was to there. It was pretty fun."

"We should do another Ontario trip sometime," Kiara said. "Go to Toronto, Ottawa, Niagara Falls..."

"Why stop there?" Bree asked. "If this road trip goes well, I say we do one across the country."

"I'm not sure we could manage that," I said slowly. A small three-week road one province over? No big deal. A road trip across one of the geographically largest countries in the world in my small SUV? That didn't seem like such a good plan.

"Well maybe not now," Harlee said. "Let's keep it in the books as a... post-graduation trip."

"Assuming we all graduate," I said wryly. Bree threw an empty pop bottle at my head.

"Ow," I said, more out of instinct than actual pain.

"Positive thoughts only," Bree said, waggling her finger in my direction. I rolled my eyes but I couldn't hold back a small laugh at her antics. "I don't understand why you're such a pessimist anyway, April."

"I'm not a pessimist," I corrected. "I'm a realist."

"You frequently go on about how the world is falling apart," Kiara said as if that proved Bree's point.

"Because it is!" I said. Harlee nodded in agreement with me but the other two looked at me doubtfully. "Whatever, we don't all have to agree. Let's get back to the road trip. Does anyone know where Elyssa is staying this month?"

"I would assume at her house," Kiara said slowly.

"Yeah, I got that," I said. "But her parents are divorced and live in different cities. Didn't she say she was switching places every month?"

"I can ask her," Bree said, grabbing her phone. "You think one of the houses is somewhere on our route?"

I frowned. Was I the only one who knew anything about Elyssa's living situation?

"Yeah, her mom lives in a cottage near Algonquin," I said. "If she's staying there, we should meet up with her."

"Oh, that would be so fun!" Kiara squealed. "Do you think she would want to join us?"

"She would only be able to come for a few days if she wanted to go back to the same house," Harlee said.

"Yeah, but if we stop by and stay at her house for a couple of days, then continue on to Algonquin, then drop her off on the way back, that would at least be a few days with her," I said. "More than we would have otherwise."

That was one of the most disappointing parts of the summer. While the four of us didn't live extremely close together, save for Harlee and Kiara of course, we were all at least within reasonable driving distance. Elyssa, on the other hand, was in an entirely different province, and we had all made our peace with the fact that we probably wouldn't get to see her at all over the summer. This, at least, provided us with a little time.

Bree's phone dinged loudly and she looked at it.

"She says she is staying with her mom for the entire month and she would love to see us," Bree said. "Should I ask her if we can stay with her for a couple of days when we get there?"

"Sure," I said.

"You should also tell her we don't have exact dates," Harlee said. "We're estimating a week and a half to get to Algonquin but there's no telling how our plans might get messed up."

Bree nodded and quickly typed out a message.

"Hopefully her mom's okay with four strangers coming to stay in her cottage."

"I've met her mom on FaceTime," I said, "I wouldn't exactly consider us strangers."

Bree laughed silently as she continued typing. "I'll be sure to mention it."

"When have you met her mom on FaceTime?" Kiara asked.

"I met her multiple times, actually," I said. "I think the first time was in September or October."

"Right, I always forget you two were roommates," Kiara said.

"That's because we all spent all our time in your room," Bree said. She set her phone down. "I sent it, I'll let you know when she responds."

"What should we do in the meantime?" Kiara asked. She grabbed a pillow from the couch and rested her chin on it.

"Maybe we should get back to our movie," I suggested. I pointed at the screen where *Legally Blonde* was still playing.

"We've missed like half an hour," Bree said, but she shifted her body so she was facing the TV instead of the small circle we had created.

"It's not like any of us haven't seen it before," Harlee said.

"But if it really bothers you, I can rewind it," I said.

Bree smiled at me knowingly. "We have missed some pretty good scenes."

I laughed and shook my head. "Guess we have to."

I pressed the rewind button and patiently waited as Kiara and Bree argued over where we had left off. I was pretty sure I knew the exact scene when our attention had been diverted to the list but I was not about to get into the middle of it.

"There!" Bree said, holding out her hand. I obligingly pressed play. She glanced at Kiara, who was frowning. "Right?"

"I'm not sure," Kiara said. "I think we might have been further in but I guess there's no harm in rewatching a little."

I put the remote down again. I subtly glanced around at my friends as the movie played. Bree's eyes were glued to the screen and she was mouthing along. When I glanced at Kiara on the other side of me, she was doing the same. I wasn't at all surprised that they both knew all the words. On the other side of Kiara, Harlee wasn't even looking at the TV screen at all. She was scrolling through Instagram and pretending that she didn't care about the movie, even though I knew she did. I smiled to myself. Even if we had only spent two weeks apart, I had missed my best friends.

5

THE NEXT NIGHT, I couldn't fall asleep. I wasn't entirely surprised at this since I'd had about three cups of coffee in the evening, and had always been very sensitive to caffeine, but it did mean that when everyone else was asleep by three a.m., I was still tossing and turning in the dark. Bree was sleeping on the air mattress, which was set up next to the couch I was laying on. When I rolled over for perhaps the fifteenth time that night, she began to stir. I froze, hoping that I did not wake her up. After a few seconds, she settled down again. As silently as possible, I slid off the couch and tiptoed down the hallway. If I couldn't sleep, I might as well go for a midnight swim. I changed into my bathing suit and went outside.

The pool and hot tub were both automatically set to light up different colours after the sun went down, so the pool was shining a beautiful purple hue and the hot tub was red.

I was originally planning to go for a proper swim, but I decided I didn't feel entirely comfortable doing so while nobody else was awake or outside with me, so I went into the hot tub instead. The hot water felt amazing in the spring air and I sighed in contentment as I sat there.

A few minutes later, the patio door opened and I just about jumped out of my skin. I quickly looked behind me to see who it was and saw Bree standing there with a bottle of wine and two glasses in her hands.

"Sorry," she said. "I didn't mean to scare you."

I shook my head. "It's fine. You didn't really."

She put the bottle and glasses down on the tile and slipped her feet into the hot tub.

"Did Elyssa make you watch that horror movie too?" She asked.

"Yes! You watched it?"

"Unfortunately yes." She smiled knowingly at me. For a brief moment, it seemed like she was going to say something else, but then she broke her gaze and gestured to the wine. "Want some?"

"Sure," I said. She poured some into both the glasses then slid one of them over to me. We clinked our glasses together before each taking a sip.

"Did you steal this from Kiara's kitchen?" I asked. It was probably a question I should have asked before taking a sip, but I hadn't thought of it until then.

"Of course not!" Bree said, looking scandalized. "I brought it with me. I thought the four of us could have it but this works too."

"Oh, so you mean you didn't plan to drink in the hot tub with me at four in the morning?"

Bree laughed. I always liked her laugh — it was real

and honest. When Bree laughed at your jokes, you knew that she meant it. My heart swelled a little at the sound.

"I love this water," Bree sighed. She moved her leg around, making the water swirl. "The colour, I mean."

"It's gorgeous," I said. "Though it is a little disconcerting to be sitting in it."

"Like sitting in a pool of blood?" Bree asked solemnly.

"Well, I— I hadn't thought about it like before, but yeah." I suddenly felt very uncomfortable in the water, as though I was actually sitting in blood. I quickly pushed myself out and sat on the side like Bree was doing.

Bree laughed. "Sorry, I didn't mean to freak you out."

I didn't want her to believe that she was the reason I got out of the water, or that I got freaked out that easily (even though she definitely already knew that), so I said, "Oh, I was just getting too warm in the water."

"Of course," she said, but it was obvious that she didn't believe me.

I looked away and drank the rest of the wine in my glass. When I put the glass back down, Bree filled it again.

"Thanks," I murmured. I took another sip, then faltered when I noticed her still half-full first glass.

"I'm not really in the mood for wine right now," she explained when she noticed my expression.

I was ready to accept that reasoning until I remembered why we had wine in the first place.

"Why did you bring it out then?" I asked. Unconsciously, I took another sip.

She shrugged. "Thought you might like it."

I stared into the water. "You didn't need to waste it on me."

"It's not a waste if you like it."

It wasn't an argument I wanted to get into at that moment, so I said nothing.

"I think I'll go for a swim," Bree said. She stood up and pulled her black dress off, revealing her bikini underneath. It was pink with little pineapples decorating it. I couldn't bite back my grin, both at the show of her personality on the bathing suit and the fact that she had thought ahead enough to put it on. She walked around the hot tub, then glanced back at me and winked. My heart skipped a beat. *Wait, what?* "Care to join me?"

"I— uh—" I stammered. I was suddenly at a loss for words and I had no idea why. I'd always known that Bree was attractive, but there was something about the way she was looking at me that felt different than before.

She tilted her head and furrowed her brows. "You okay, April? You look a little sick."

I blinked a couple of times and swallowed, trying to force myself to look normal again. I shook my head.

"I'm fine," I said. I took another sip of wine as I tried to think of an excuse to give her. "I don't really feel like swimming right now. I'm... a little tipsy."

I actually wasn't feeling the effect of the wine at all yet but it was the best excuse I could think of. I tried to convince myself that it was true and that it was causing the butterflies that had suddenly erupted in my stomach.

"Okay," Bree said with a small shrug. She ran daintily down the deck and dove into the pool. She disappeared under the water for nearly a minute then reappeared on the opposite end of the pool with a laugh. The purple lights shone brightly against her wet skin. I felt like I had swallowed my tongue. "The water is such a nice temperature, April!"

She started swimming on her back. I watched her, mesmerized. Water dripped down her long, toned arms as she brought them out of the water. Her eyes were closed as she kicked lazily, giving off the impression that this was the most relaxing activity in the world for her. I realized my mouth was hanging open as I looked at her, and I forced myself to close it.

Where the hell did this come from? Maybe I should quit drinking.

I put my wine glass down beside me and tried to focus on anything but Bree in the water. Unfortunately, whenever I tried to force myself not to do something, it was all I wanted to do, and I continuously found my eyes drifting back towards her. All I wanted to do was jump in and join her, but I knew that was a terrible plan. After about ten minutes of swimming, which felt like an eternity to me, she stopped and came over to stand by the edge of the pool.

"I wish I had a pool," she sighed. I nodded in agreement but couldn't bring myself to say anything in response. Bree continued talking, she was always very good at filling silences, and I followed along as best I could, but there was only one thought running through my mind: *I have to be over this by the morning. I cannot fall for her.*

❧ 6 ❧

THE SUN WAS bright the next morning and I hated it. An unfortunate side effect of having a much younger sister at home was that she got up at the crack of dawn and expected me to do the same, so I had gotten in the habit of waking up very early, even when I stayed up late. Which meant that I found myself exhausted, hungover, and awake before any of my friends.

I experimentally groaned and stretched. I was sore, even though I had done nothing the night before to cause that, and my head was pounding. At first, I didn't want to get up, but a wave of nausea came over me, and I didn't really want to risk throwing up while lying right next to Bree.

I dragged myself off the couch and stumbled down the hall to the bathroom. Without turning on the light, I dropped onto the blissfully cool tile floor and sighed.

I will never drink again.

I told myself that every time I drank and as expected, I broke it every time. It was my own fault, really. After she got out of the pool, Bree and I finished off the bottle of wine. Neither of us were tired enough to sleep yet, so we grabbed the bottle of vodka I had brought along for the weekend that we hadn't used, and did a few shots. Evidently, that was not a good plan.

I wanted to shower before anyone else woke up, so once I was pretty sure that I wasn't going to throw up, I forced myself to stand again. The world spun around me a little. I blindly reached out for the shower handle and turned it. As the water warmed up, I turned on the lights. The brightness made the pounding in my head begin anew.

Okay, this time I really mean it. I will never drink again.

I knew that feeling wasn't going to last but it made me feel better to at least try and convince myself that this would be the last hangover I ever experienced.

That was probably the slowest shower that I ever took, given how hard I was finding it to lift my arms beyond shoulder height. As I showered, I tried to remember the events of the night before a little more. I remembered the drinking and Bree swimming and then the drinking again, but I couldn't remember anything beyond that. That seemed like it should have been the only important parts of the night, a general overview of them at least, but there was a nagging feeling in the back of my mind, telling me I was forgetting something important.

And that something important hit me in the face when I saw a glimpse of Bree's bathing suit hanging in the bathroom.

Shit.

It had to be the alcohol. That was the only explanation for me suddenly being attracted to Bree. There couldn't be anything else to it. I mean sure, I had thought about it a couple of times before, but never really seriously. We had joked about it during some of those late nights in residence, when we were all hanging out in Kiara and Harlee's room. One of us would go on some terrible date and we would say *we should just date each other* or *we'll probably end up together one day, huh?* But then we would laugh it off because it wasn't serious. Nothing was ever serious between Bree and me.

I finished getting ready, at least as best I could in the state that I was, and I walked back out to the main area of the basement, where Kiara, Harlee and Bree were just starting to get up. Everything was normal at first. But then, I made the mistake of looking at Bree. She smiled at me. Her kind smile that absolutely lit up her face. My heart started beating faster. Butterflies erupted in my stomach. I almost dropped the clothes I was holding in my arms but I tightened my grip at the last second.

"We were wondering where you got to," Bree said. "How did you wake up so early?"

"I..." *Do I know how to speak? How the hell do people speak?* "I had to get a shower in before you guys stole it."

"You better not have used up all the hot water," Kiara said, pointing a hairbrush in my direction. I just shook my head.

I was still standing pretty far from them, which I was honestly okay with, given the alternative was standing right next to Bree, but Harlee was giving me a weird look so I forced my feet to move forward. I walked around the far side of the couch so I wouldn't have to brush by

Bree and tried to keep my distance as much as possible as I put my pyjamas away.

"Hungover?" Bree asked me quietly. I just nodded, not trusting myself to speak. I think she figured out that I wasn't really in the mood to talk, although probably for a reason different to mine. She just lightly brushed her hand against my shoulder in what I think was meant to be a comforting gesture, but really it just made the butterflies erupt anew, then walked away.

"I call this shower!" Harlee called, just as she closed the bathroom door shut.

"You can use the upstairs shower if you want," Kiara said to Bree. "I'll go after you."

"Thanks," Bree said. She ran upstairs. My shoulders slumped in relief. I sat on the couch and put my head in my hands. *What have I done?*

"I'm going to make some coffee," Kiara said. "You want to come up with me?"

"I'll be there in a minute," I said. I lifted my head again. "I want to finish packing first."

"You can do that later," Kiara said. "You're welcome to stay the whole day."

I forced a polite smile. Admittedly, I was originally going to stay until the evening, but with everything going on in my brain, I wanted to get out of there as soon as possible. I wasn't sure when I would get a chance to do so, but I didn't want to be held up by an unpacked bag.

"Thanks, but I'd rather be prepared."

"Okay." She went upstairs. I sighed and looked around at my stuff. I didn't have that much stuff strewn about the room, but it looked overwhelming at that moment. I allowed myself another minute to just sit and stew and question everything I was feeling, then I forced myself to stand up and start putting things away. Kiara was bound to get suspicious if I took too long.

Once I finished, I headed upstairs. Apparently, I took longer than I thought I did, because she had already made coffee and was in the middle of making some pancakes. I usually didn't like to eat the morning after drinking but the smell of food was intoxicating.

Kiara glanced at me over her shoulder.

"Hey," she said. She pointed at a mug on the island. "I poured you some coffee with cream. That's how you like it right?"

I nodded, then regretted that decision as my vision swam. I swallowed thickly.

"Yeah, it is. Thanks." I sat down on a barstool and took a couple of sips of the drink.

"Pancakes will be ready in a few."

A couple of minutes later, Harlee came running up the stairs. She was dressed in a tank top and shorts, and her straight hair was left wet.

"Smells good, Kiara!" She said. She grabbed some plates and cutlery for us and put them on the counter. Kiara dumped some pancakes on each of our plates.

"Eat up," she said. She didn't need to tell me twice. I inhaled two pancakes before Harlee had even finished her first.

"You're hungry this morning," Harlee commented mildly.

I shrugged. "Yeah."

"Hey guys," Bree said as she walked into the kitchen. She sat down on the other side of me. The smell of her strawberry shampoo was intoxicating. "Thanks for cooking, Kiara."

"It's no problem," Kiara said. She put two pancakes on a plate and slid it over to Bree.

"This is definitely going to sound weird," Harlee said, "but I love the smell of your shampoo, Bree."

I was glad I wasn't the only one who thought it.

Bree laughed. "Thank you, it's new."

I wanted to echo Harlee's sentiments but the thought of saying something like that to Bree made my heart pound a little too fast in my chest so I stayed quiet.

"So, what do you guys want to do today?" Kiara asked. Across from us, she leaned against the island and began eating her own breakfast. "I think my parents will be back around dinnertime."

I cleared my throat. "I think I'm actually going to leave soon," I said. I tried to think of a plausible excuse off the top of my head that wasn't *I'm scared I'm going to kiss Bree or some shit*. "I told Jeanie I would pick her up from school, and I want to make sure I leave myself enough time to get home."

It wasn't a lie, exactly. Jean liked it when I picked her up from school when I was home and wasn't working. She hadn't specifically asked me to do so today, but I knew she would really appreciate it.

Harlee laughed and shook her head. "See, you can try all you want to pretend you're this stoic and uncaring person, but we all know you're a big softie."

"I am not!" I said. "It's just that Jeanie is an exception."

They all laughed. I clearly hadn't convinced them but I found I didn't mind too much.

"Are you sure you don't want to stay?" Bree asked as I slammed the trunk closed.

"I'm going to see you guys again in a week," I said. "We're going on a road trip, remember?"

"But a week is so long!" Bree cried melodramatically, falling against me. And I don't mean just lightly falling — that girl dropped her entire body weight on me like she fainted. I stumbled a bit as she hit me but luckily I was used to her antics and was able to catch her before we both fell over.

"I think you'll live," I said. I kept my calm exterior as always, though my heart was singing on the inside.

That's not how you feel about your other friends.

"We'll see you next week, April," Kiara said. She opened the car door for me and I climbed inside. "Say hi to your family for us."

"I will," I said, even though none of them knew my family. I slammed the door shut and put the car in reverse. Bree and Kiara backed away. I slowly pulled out of the driveway and onto the street. Once I put the car back into drive mode, I waved at them out the window.

"Text us when you get home!" Bree called after me. I shot her a thumbs up and drove off.

As I PACKED LATER that week, I mused over my feelings about going on a trip with a girl that I so clearly had feelings for. A girl who also so happened to be one of my best friends in the world.

It was an awful idea if I'd ever heard one.

At the same time, though, I wanted to go. I had already committed to finishing everything on the list, even if the commitment was only in my mind, and this was probably the only chance I would get to do so before my twentieth birthday. Besides, the other three were looking forward to the road trip as well, and I didn't want to bail on them. And did I really want to give up this amazing opportunity on the off chance that these feelings might be something serious? What if it was just some sort of short-term thing, an infatuation of sorts that would go away as quickly as it appeared? In fact, that was almost definitely what it was. And not going on the road would be the worst course of action to take based on that.

I threw down the clothes I had been failing at folding for the past ten minutes and looked over the list again. I wasn't a hugely sentimental person. I had a couple of things from my childhood and teen years that I kept, but only a couple. As a whole, I didn't hold onto things that didn't serve a purpose to me. But when I looked at this list, all I could remember was how much hope I had put into the future. I was very unhappy and had been told at every turn that life would get better, so I wrote myself a list of things that I wanted to do — at the time, I thought that if I managed to do all these things by the time I was twenty, then it would mean that I was happy. My logic didn't exactly check out, but I liked the idea of fulfilling that naive dream.

I had to go on this trip. I just had to find a way to avoid Bree and my complicated feelings for her while I was on it. How hard could that be?

❧ 8 ❧

FOR THE FIRST leg of the trip, I had to drive alone. I was meeting Bree, Kiara, and Harlee in East Port since it was the most central town. It felt pointless to drive back there only a week after leaving, but it made the most logistical sense.

Unfortunately, my morning did not start well. I barely slept the night before, my coffee machine wouldn't work so I was under-caffeinated, and Jean had hidden my car keys as some sort of game before she left for school. Do you know where I found them? Under her dresser, all the way against the wall. I had to move the whole thing to get them out.

But still, despite these hiccups, I tried to look on the bright side of things. There was a Tim Hortons on the way to East Port, so I stopped to get coffee and break-fast, which at least put me in a moderately good mood.

While I drove the rest of the way, I told myself that everything was going to go well for the trip. Bree always went on and on about how we attract the energy we put into the world, which I always thought was bullshit, but I was willing to do anything if it meant this whole idea wouldn't immediately blow up in my face. So by the time I reached Harlee's house, I was feeling good about this whole idea.

Of course, all my hopes crashed and burned very quickly.

Kiara and Harlee were sitting on the front porch of Harlee's house when I pulled up.

"Hey guys," I said, jumping out of my car. "Bree's not here yet?"

Harlee shook her head. "She had to take the bus here, and it got delayed."

"Okay," I said. That made sense. While Bree was the one who used the truck the most, I could definitely understand why her family wouldn't want her to leave it at Harlee's place for three weeks while we were gone. I figured while we waited for her, we could figure out some logistical things, though. "So, I was thinking that I could drive the first leg of the trip, then we could switch after a couple of hours. And maybe we just have two people drive every day so we only have to drive every other day. How does that sound?"

"Oh," was all Kiara said. She and Harlee glanced at each other awkwardly. My heart sank.

"Oh?" I asked. "What's 'oh'?"

"Don't get mad," Kiara said slowly. *Well, that's never a good thing to hear.* "But neither of us have our driver's licenses."

It took a moment for my brain to catch up with what she meant. But when it did, I just about exploded.

"What do you mean neither of you have your driver's license?" I all but yelled.

"Sorry," Kiara said sheepishly. "I didn't think it was important."

"We're going on a road trip!" I was definitely yelling now. "We are going on a road trip and you didn't think having your fucking driver's license was important?"

"Bree has a license," Harlee added, as if I hadn't already known that. "And she'll probably be fine with driving your car."

"She better." I crossed my arms and turned away from them, muttering under my breath about the ridiculousness of them never mentioning they couldn't drive before we left on a road trip. After a minute, I turned back to them and pointed an accusing finger in their direction. "I swear, if that girl shows up here and tells me she can't drive my car, we're not even leaving this driveway! You got it?"

Both of them nodded with wide eyes. I sighed and turned away from them again. I didn't mean to snap at them like that; I just would have appreciated a heads up about all of this. I bit my nails and paced like a caged tiger in front of them as we waited for Bree. Although I knew it probably wasn't her fault she was late, I found myself getting incredibly frustrated waiting for her. I checked my watch about every five seconds.

Finally, after about ten minutes, fast footsteps approached behind me. I looked back and saw Bree running in our direction, her big duffel bag swinging by her side. She skidded to a stop at the end of Harlee's driveway.

"Sorry I'm late," she said breathlessly. "For some

reason, there was traffic when I left my house even though it was like five in the morning, so I missed the bus I was supposed to take and had to wait thirty minutes for the next one, and then I ran all the way here but I guess I wasn't fast enough and..." She cut off her rambling and smiled apologetically. "Sorry. I hope you weren't waiting for too long."

Although I had been ready to bite someone's head off a minute ago, all my anger dissipated when I looked at Bree.

"It's fine," I said. I clasped my hands together in front of me in some sort of semi-prayer. "Just please tell me you are all right with driving my car."

"Yeah, of course!" Bree said with a happy nod. She glanced over the group of us, her smile slowly slipping away. "Is anyone else?"

"Harlee and Kiara don't have their driver's licenses," I said.

Bree shifted her bag on her shoulder.

"Oh." She looked at me again. "So it's just going to be the two of us driving. The whole time."

The anger was welling up in my chest again at the entire set of circumstances and I tried to push it back down.

"Yeah," I said flatly. "It's going to be so fun."

Kiara smiled apologetically.

"I'm really sorry about this, guys," she said. "It never really occurred to me that you guys didn't know."

"It's fine!" Bree said in her typical happy voice. She wasn't one to get angry or hold a grudge. "It just took us by surprise."

"Let's get going," I said. "Better to get a headstart on the day."

"I'll drive first," Bree offered.

"Oh, I don't mind driving first," I said. I glanced behind Bree; Harlee and Kiara were whispering to each other, and it made me worried that they were planning something.

"No, you've already been driving all morning," Bree said. "I'll take the first shift."

I didn't care enough to argue with her so I conceded. Harlee and Kiara went quiet and turned to me.

"You sit up front," Harlee said to me. I frowned. It wasn't that I didn't like sitting in the passenger seat, but based on the times I had driven with them, Kiara and Harlee always fought over who got shotgun in the car. There had to be some angle or caveat to her offer.

"Why?" I asked warily.

"We feel bad that we can't drive," Kiara said. "So, we think it's only fair that you guys get to sit up front for the whole drive."

"Oh, that's sweet," Bree said.

"But unnecessary," I added quickly. My entire plan for the trip was to avoid being alone or too close to Bree. Sitting beside her for hours every day wasn't exactly the best way to go about that.

"We insist," Harlee said firmly.

"And," Kiara said before I could get a word in edgewise, "like you said, we need to get going so we don't have time to argue about it."

I narrowed my eyes. I didn't appreciate her using my words against me, but she did have a point.

"We'll talk about it later," I said finally. Kiara grinned

as though she had just won the argument and got in the car. I didn't understand why she was so happy, seeing as the deal wasn't exactly great for her.

Not dwelling on the matter, I got in the car as well and passed the keys over to Bree, who was sitting in the driver's seat. I watched her somewhat warily as she started the car and put it in drive, unsure of how confident she was in driving my car, but she seemed very comfortable with the whole thing, which put my mind at ease, at least a little.

"This is going to be so fun guys!" Bree said. Then she slammed on the gas and away we went.

❧ 9 ❧

WE HAD ALL gotten up early for this trip, so for the first couple of hours, the car was silent as we gradually woke up for the day. Or, in Harlee and Kiara's case, took a nap until it was an 'appropriate time to be awake'.

I was apparently the only one who had thought to eat breakfast, so we stopped at another Tim Hortons to get food for everyone else. Since we were there anyway, I got a coffee for myself anyway. After that stop, everyone was much more energetic. I couldn't decide whether that was a good thing or a bad thing — I felt a little like a parent driving my kids somewhere, who just wants some peace and quiet.

"Hey, Kiara," Bree asked, once we were about thirty minutes away from the Tim's. "Did you ever tell your parents that you're leaving?"

I turned around in my seat so I could see Kiara, who was sitting behind Bree. Her eyes widened in shock at the question, which I took as a resounding no, she did not tell them.

"I totally forgot about that!" Kiara said. She whipped her phone out of her bag. "Thanks for reminding me."

"Are you going to call them now?" Harlee asked.

"I was just planning on texting them," Kiara said. She looked up from her phone. "Why, do you think I should call them?"

"They would probably appreciate it," Harlee said dryly. "Can you imagine getting a text from your daughter saying 'I'm on a road trip, I'll see you in three weeks'?"

Kiara bit her lip. "Yeah, I guess that's not the best plan..."

Her mind made up, she pressed the call button and held her phone to her ear. There was an awkward silence as she waited for somebody to pick up. A moment later, I could just barely hear the muffled sound of her mother saying, "Hello?"

"Uh, hey mom," Kiara said. "So don't be angry but I'm actually going to be gone for a little longer than I thought."

There were some more unintelligible sounds from the phone.

"How long?" She scratched her nose. "Oh, just, you know, three weeks."

Her mother's screech of "Three weeks?" was loud and clear, even though I was nowhere near the phone. Kiara cringed and held the phone away from her ear a little.

"Yeah," she said. "We decided to go on a road trip. It was a bit of a spontaneous decision, really. Anyway, I definitely won't be gone for more than three weeks."

Her mother seemed to have calmed down at least a little because her words were unintelligible to me again.

"Where are we going?" Kiara asked. She bit her lip. For a moment, I wondered whether she was going to lie, or at least stretch the truth, like she had when she said the road trip was supposedly 'spontaneous'. "Just to, uh, Ontario. Algonquin to be exact."

And the screeching was back. I still couldn't make heads or tails of what she was saying, but this time it was because of how fast she was ranting rather than the volume. Kiara put her microphone on mute so her mother wouldn't be able to hear us speak.

"And this is why I didn't want to do this over the phone," she said.

Harlee laughed. "This is exactly why I wanted you to do this on the phone."

Kiara glared at her. "Do you enjoy watching my suffering?"

"Of course," Harlee said dismissively.

"How long do you think she's going to keep yelling?" Bree asked, looking at Kiara in the rearview mirror.

Kiara shrugged. "In my experience, she can go on forever. But if it's distracting you, I can hang up."

I raised my eyebrows. "You're going to hang up on your mother while she's screaming at you?"

"Yeah, why not?" Kiara asked. She grinned. "I'm going to be gone for the next three weeks anyway, then I'll only be home for two weeks before I leave to work at camp. Doesn't leave her a lot of time to be mad."

"I don't know that that's a good idea," I said, but Kiara waved me off.

She unmuted the phone and held it to her ear again. From what I could tell, her mother was still ranting at her but Kiara just said, "Sorry mom, I have to go!" and hung up the phone before she could react.

"She's going to kill you when you get home," Harlee said. "Even if you're only home for two weeks."

"That's a problem for future me," Kiara said. She dropped her phone on the seat beside her. "Anyway, at least that's done for now. Should we put on some music?"

I was a little surprised by how nonchalant she was being about the whole thing but as someone who was also a big believer in the 'that's a problem for future me' philosophy, I didn't push it.

"Sure," I said. "Anyone have a good playlist?"

"I do," Bree said. "I made one for the trip. I think everyone will like it."

"Aw, she made us a playlist," Kiara said in a fake sweet voice. Bree's face heated up a little.

"I didn't want us to have to argue over whose music to play," she said.

"Don't worry Bree, I think it's sweet," I said. I plugged the aux cord into her phone and opened Spotify. "What's the playlist called?"

"Songs to commit crimes to," she said nonchalantly. My finger from over the screen and I looked up at her.

"What?" I asked.

"What? You know I like to give my playlists weird names."

"Yeah, but I wouldn't have expected that name from you. Harlee, maybe, but not you."

She shrugged and glanced at me before looking at the road again.

"Like I said, you guys are changing me."

Harlee leaned forward.

"For better or for worse," she said, and pressed play.

10

ON THE SECOND day of the trip, we got caught in an awful rainstorm. At first, it was only light rain but it picked up in intensity very quickly until the point that I almost couldn't see anything.

"I think there's a diner coming up on the right!" Bree said. "Let's just stop for lunch and wait the rain out."

I nodded in agreement. I didn't want to drive in this weather for any longer than I had to and we needed to stop for food anyway. I slowed down even more than before to make absolutely sure that I wouldn't miss the turn.

In other circumstances, I might have considered the diner to be a little sketchy since it was the only building on the long stretch of highway but there were many cars parked outside it, and I could see people happily chatting and eating inside as well, so I told myself we were unlikely to get murdered. Even then, I probably wouldn't have stopped there if it hadn't been such bad weather, but beggars can't be choosers. I parked in what seemed to be a parking spot, although it was a gravel parking lot without any spaces clearly marked, and killed the engine.

The rain sounded louder without the engine running. I squinted outside and sighed. It didn't look like it was going to stop any time soon and we didn't have any umbrellas or rain jackets that were easily accessible as far as I knew.

"Should we run for it?" I asked.

"I guess we don't have much of a choice," Bree said.

"Wait," Harlee said. I looked back. "Isn't 'dance in the rain' one of the things on your list?"

"Yeah," I said. I looked outside again. "But I was thinking more of a light rain instead of a torrential downpour."

"Let's just do it now!" Harlee said. "It will be nice to cross something off the list, don't you think?"

I frowned. "I don't know, Harlee..."

"What do you guys think?" Harlee asked.

"We might as well," Kiara said. I wasn't surprised that she agreed with Harlee; the two of them seemed to have the same mind most of the time. I turned to Bree, who was now my last hope. I wouldn't be able to argue against all three of them but if Bree didn't want to do it either, then it would be split either way.

Bree looked uneasily between me and Harlee. I was sure we both had very determined looks on our faces.

"Um...I guess we can do it?" She said, her voice rising in pitch with every word.

"Bree," I whined, while Harlee said, "Yes!"

"You don't have to if you don't want to, April," Bree reassured me. She placed her hand lightly on my wrist. I instantly felt sparks. I almost pulled away but managed to stop myself. I didn't want to accidentally hurt her feelings.

"I'm not going to stay in the car if you're all going out," I said. What would be the point of that? I unlocked my door. "Whatever. Come on."

Harlee leapt out of the car immediately, as if this was the most fun thing in the world. The rest of us climbed out at a much slower pace. The rain was coming down so heavily that it actually hurt my head slightly when it landed.

"Guess we won't need to shower tonight," Bree said with a laugh. She pushed her long hair out of her face.

I shook my head. My hair was already soaked and rain droplets were running down my face.

"No, definitely not."

"Come on, guys!" Kiara called. She began spinning in a circle, causing her skirt to flare out a little even though it was wet. I laughed. I held my arms out to the side, leaned my head back and spun around as well.

For those few seconds, I felt like a kid again.

After I spun around like that for a little while, I got too dizzy to continue and dropped my arms back down to my sides. The world was rocking like a boat and I stumbled to the person closest to me, who happened to be Bree. We knocked into each other, and both laughed.

Kiara and Harlee ran over to join us a moment later. Now that I wasn't moving around, I was getting a little cold and crossed my arms over my chest.

We stood in a huddled group near the edge of the parking lot. I considered suggesting that we move under the overhang by the entrance to the restaurant since the rain was still pouring down around us, but I decided it wasn't really worth it, given that we were already soaked. If we stood over there, anyone in the restaurant would be able to see us, unlike where we were already.

"Should we get food now?" Kiara asked.

"You want to go into a restaurant looking like this?" I asked in disbelief.

"Well, we need to eat and we can't drive in this weather," Kiara said. "What else do you want to do?"

"That's a good point," Bree said. "We either have to sit in the car or the restaurant if we want to get out of the rain."

I did have to concede to that point. I would have just said that we should sit in the car and not embarrass ourselves further, but I didn't want to get my car seats wet, and I was pretty sure all of our towels were packed deep in the bags.

"So, who's going to go in and ask for a table?" Kiara asked. We all exchanged glances, but nobody said anything.

"Nose goes," I said. I quickly put my finger on my nose. The other three did the same so quickly that I wasn't entirely sure who was last.

"I think that was Kiara," Bree said.

"What?" Kiara asked. "It was not! Besides, April didn't give us any warning, so it should be her!"

"No chance in hell," I said. "I was against us going out in the rain in the first place."

"Well I'm not doing it," Kiara said, crossing her arms over her chest. She was incredibly stubborn and arguing with her would mean being outside for even longer so I went along with it.

"Fine, that leaves Bree and Harlee, then," I said. Neither of them looked very happy about that prospect.

"Rock, paper, scissors?" Bree suggested. Harlee nodded, a frown on her face.

"Wait, is it one round or best two out of three?" I asked. It was always best to decide on the rules beforehand. Otherwise, the loser of the first round would say they're doing best two out of three, while the winner would say it was one round only.

"One round?" Bree suggested. Harlee shrugged, which was her way of saying 'sure'.

"I'll call it," Kiara said. "Rock, paper, scissors, shoot!"

Bree did a rock, while Harlee did scissors.

"Ha!" Bree said, lightly hitting Harlee's hand with her fist. "I win."

"Okay," Harlee sighed. I didn't say it out loud but I thought it was best that Harlee was the one to go in. As much as I hated to admit it, she was better than any of us at seeming like something didn't bother her at all, and that was a skill that would prove useful in this situation.

We walked over to the entrance of the diner with her but remained outside while she walked in. Through the windows, I could see her talking with the hostess for a few moments. Luckily, it seemed like they weren't immediately telling her to leave.

Soon, Harlee waved at us to come inside. The waitress, Olivia, did look at us a little oddly but she didn't say anything as she grabbed four menus and led us to a booth in the back corner of the restaurant. I slid into the far side of the booth, which was rather uncomfortable to do in wet clothing. Bree sat next to me. I hoped that she didn't notice me awkwardly shift to the side so there was a little more space between us than she left initially.

"I'll let you look over the menu for a few minutes," Olivia said. She walked off.

"Are we sitting under a vent?" Kiara asked. She looked at the ceiling and frowned. "I'm freezing."

"You know, it just occurred to me that we all have dry clothes in the car," Bree said. "We could have brought them in and gotten changed in the bathroom."

We all stared at her.

"Why would you say that?" I asked. "Why would you say that after we already sat down and made the whole booth wet?"

"Sorry," Bree grinned.

"Hey, I have an idea for a game we could play," Harlee said, tapping her fingernails on the table. "Well, maybe it's not entirely a game. I'm not sure."

"A game that's not really a game," Kiara said. "I'm intrigued."

Harlee opened a webpage on her phone and put it down on the table so we could all see. It was a list of questions.

"They're questions to help you get to know someone on a more personal level," Harlee said. "We go around the circle and ask the person sitting to our right any question off this list. For example, Kiara, what age do you feel on the inside?"

"Oh," Kiara said. She chewed on her lip as she thought. "Probably about seven years old."

"As someone who has known you since you were seven years old, I can safely say you have not changed much," Harlee said. She handed the phone over to me. "Now, you pick a question to ask me."

"Okay..." I said. I glanced over the list of questions. "Harlee, what is your greatest fear?"

"Easy," Harlee said. "Cannibalism."

That was definitely not the answer I had been expecting, but she said it with such a straight face that I was sure she meant it.

"In what context?" Bree asked slowly.

Harlee's eyebrows pulled together. "What do you mean in what context? I'm just scared of cannibalism, plain and simple."

"Okay, yeah, but do you mean like you're scared of being in a position where you have to eat someone else? Or are you scared of a serial killer killing you so they can eat your body?"

"All of the above. Anything that involves a human eating another human being." She squirmed. "It freaks me out."

Until that moment, I had never thought of Harlee as somebody who had any fears. Of course, I knew that everyone was afraid of something, but she had always been so cool and collected that I couldn't imagine her being afraid of anything. To see her so disconcerted by the mere idea of cannibalism felt wrong in some way.

Bree cleared her throat. "All right, next question. April, who do you like the most out of all of us?"

"What?" I asked. I tried to grab the phone back from her but she held it out of reach. "That is definitely not a question on the list."

"You can't prove that," Bree said stubbornly.

"I'm sure I can prove it pretty easily," I said. I went to grab the phone again but she just leaned back, and soon it became an all-out war. Unfortunately, due to this, none of us noticed Olivia walking back over to our table to take our order. As such, right as Olivia arrived and opened her mouth, Kiara (quite loudly) said, "Can we come back to cannibalism for a second? I have questions."

"What kind of questions could you possibly have?" Harlee asked, in a tone that clearly showed how stupid she thought the statement was. "It's cannibalism. One person eats another. Simple."

Olivia cleared her throat. I froze in place, which at that moment happened to be me almost lying on top of Bree, who was pretty much hanging off the bench with her arm hanging out so I couldn't get the phone. How she didn't notice that her head was at Olivia's feet is beyond me. I slowly lifted my head. Olivia was staring straight at me, a look of utter confusion and horror on her face.

"Hello," I said in as normal of a tone I could manage. I slowly pushed myself back up to a seated position and grabbed Bree's hand to pull her up as well. Once we were all in our regular positions, I pushed my wet hair out of my face and looked around the table. It seemed nobody else was going to say anything so I said, "Sorry about that. What's going on?" I cringed immediately after saying it. I was pretty sure that wasn't something a normal person would say to their server.

"I was just wondering if you were ready to order," Olivia said in a strained voice. Man, she probably thought we were about to suggest that we wanted to eat a person. Or that we were some sort of serial killing team, here to kill everyone in the restaurant.

Luckily, we all had our orders prepared and we said them quickly. Olivia nodded quickly, stammered out that it would be ready soon, and ran off.

"How did none of us notice her standing there?" Bree moaned, hiding her face in her hands.

"It wasn't so bad," Harlee said. "I'm sure they get a lot of weird customers in here."

"I guess..." Bree said, though she didn't seem thoroughly convinced.

"Why don't we just move on to the next question?" I suggested. Bree passed the phone over to Kiara, who was sitting across from her. She scrolled down the page.

"Bree, if there were twenty-six hours in a day instead of twenty-four, what would you do more of?"

"I guess whatever my main hobby is at that time," Bree said. "At the moment, I guess I would spend more time with friends."

"What, being with us twenty-four hours a day right now isn't enough for you?" I asked in a deadpan voice.

Bree laughed. "I meant in general. But if you're going to be like that, then maybe I will say that I would spend those extra two hours sleeping."

"That's a much better answer," I said with a nod. Kiara passed the phone to Harlee.

"Oh, I like this one!" Harlee said. "Kiara, how do you think you will die?"

"I'm starting to get scared that you will kill and eat me," Kiara said immediately. Bree and I laughed, while Harlee hit her with the dessert menu over and over.

"I said I was scared of cannibalism, not that I would partake in it!"

"Okay, I'm sorry, I'm sorry!" Kiara said. Harlee pulled back and tossed the menu back on the table. "Anyway, I'm interested in your guys' answers to the questions. Bree, how do you think you will die?"

Bree's eyes widened in mild panic. "I would rather not consider it."

"Yeah, fair enough," Kiara said. "How about you, April?"

"I plan to never die."

"Yeah, that checks out," Harlee said. She slid the phone over to me. "Your turn to choose."

"Okay." I decided to pick one that I was pretty sure wouldn't end up with an answer like 'cannibalism'. "What does your name mean?"

She grimaced. "It means 'hare meadow'."

"Oh," I said. That was a strange name meaning if I'd ever heard one and I wasn't quite sure how to respond. After a moment, I just handed the phone to Bree.

"All right, April, I already somewhat know the answer to this one—"

"Then why ask it?"

"Hush. What tattoos do you have and what are their meanings or significance to you?"

I rolled my eyes. They all knew that I had tattoos but I had never told them what they meant to me. It wasn't so much that I wanted to keep them a secret, as much as I just didn't like talking about myself very much.

"I have this flower," I said. I lifted my T-shirt sleeve to show the violet on my left upper arm. "I got this just after my grandmother's death when I was sixteen, because violets are considered a sign of woman-loving woman, and she was a lesbian."

"She was?" Harlee asked in surprise. That was most people's reactions when I told them. It wasn't common to hear about people in older generations being out with their sexualities.

"Yeah. She really helped me with accepting my sexuality and coming out." While it had been a few years since she had passed, I still missed her greatly and didn't want to dwell on the matter for long. "And, uh, the other tattoo is on my ribcage, I'm sure you guys have seen it. It says 'someone, I tell you, in another time will remember us'. It's a quote by Sappho."

"So what you're saying is that both your tattoos are gay," Bree said.

"Did you really expect anything different?"

"From you?" Harlee asked. "Never."

Kiara grabbed the phone next. "Okay, Bree. What are you most grateful for in the world?"

Bree thought for a moment then said very seriously, "Titties."

I almost spat out the drink that I was in the middle of sipping. I should have expected the answer, of course, given the friends I was sitting with, but it still took me by surprise.

Harlee smiled. "Yours or someone else's?"

"Both, of course."

"Sorry to interrupt," Olivia said awkwardly. For the second time during that conversation, I choked on my water. Based on the looks of surprise and embarrassment donning my friends' faces, none of them had noticed Olivia standing there either. That girl had a gift of invisibility or something. I just hoped she hadn't been there for long, but based on the look on her face, she had heard the whole interaction. "Here's your food. I, uh, hope you enjoy."

She ran off immediately.

"Oops," Bree said.

"We should really stop talking," Kiara said.

"It's fine, it's fine," Harlee said. "We'll leave a good tip, and never under any circumstances visit this town again. Agreed?"

"Agreed," we all said simultaneously.

11

IT WAS LATE by the time we got to a motel that night, and we were all exhausted. The night before, our motel room only had two double beds. I had shared with Kiara, and Harlee had shared with Bree. For a group of four people, two beds worked perfectly. None of us minded sharing the beds, and it was cheaper than getting two rooms. But the second night, the manager of the hotel so graciously offered us an extra cot, so only two people would have to share a bed. I knew she meant well by doing so but it ultimately just caused more problems than solutions — because it forced us to decide who had to share a bed.

"I've been driving all day," I argued. "In the rain! Don't you think I deserve a good night's rest?"

"Okay, but Bree has also been driving in the rain," Kiara said. "And the cot isn't nearly as comfortable as a bed so only one of you will get to sleep alone in the good bed, and how is that fair?"

"What would you suggest, then?"

"Glad you asked!" She said. "I'll take the cot because I'm used to sleeping on uncomfortable beds at camp—"

"It doesn't actually look that uncomfortable," Harlee said, looking over the cot appraisingly.

"Trust me, you would eat your words once you spent a night in it," Kiara said. "So, I'll take the cot. And the three of you can divide up the beds however you want."

"This feels like your way of avoiding sharing a bed with anyone," Bree said suspiciously.

"Moi?" Kiara asked, putting a hand to her chest. "Why, I would never manipulate you like that!"

Harlee threw a pillow at her.

"As idiotic as Kiara is," Harlee said, "she does have a point. She can sleep anywhere, and won't complain in the morning if her back hurts. So that leaves the three of us. How do we want to divide it?"

"Do you still kick in your sleep, Harlee?" I asked. I'd only slept in the same bed as Harlee once, in a situation similar to this, and I woke up with bruises on my legs the next morning. I'm not sure I even slept an hour in that whole night.

"She does," Bree said. "Trust me."

I figured Bree was the most likely to know, given that she had shared a bed with Harlee the night before.

"Yeah, sorry about that," Harlee said. "Kiara is my only friend who doesn't mind it."

"I can sleep through anything," Kiara said. "Including Harlee trying to break my legs in her sleep."

"Okay, I do not kick you that hard!"

"How would you know?"

"Anyway," Bree said loudly before that could turn into a full-scale argument. "I think it's probably easiest is

April and I share a bed, so we can actually get some sleep tonight. I don't think anyone wants us falling asleep at the wheel."

"Definitely not," Harlee agreed.

If I had thought through how this conversation was bound to go, I wouldn't have mentioned Harlee kicking in her sleep. In fact, I would have taken sharing a bed with her and dealing with the bruises for the next few days over having to share a bed with the girl that I was secretly into. Unfortunately, I did not think that far ahead and I had no possible excuse for not wanting to share a bed with Bree that wouldn't hurt her feelings.

"All right it's settled then," Bree said. I opened my mouth to argue, to say absolutely anything, even *I'll just sleep on the floor* but she ploughed on before I got the chance. "April and I will take this bed, Harlee will take that one, and Kiara will take the cot."

There was no possible way for me to argue against it at that point. I was screwed.

Bree was already in bed scrolling on her phone when I finished brushing my teeth ten minutes later and came back into the room. As casually as possible, I slipped into the bed, *lying right next to her*, and shifted as close to the edge of the bed as I could get without falling off of it. I idly wondered if there was some non-suspicious way of me suggesting that we split the bed down the middle with pillows so that we didn't accidentally touch in the night, but that would definitely be a red flag that some-thing was up. Friends shared beds all the time. Hell, Bree and I had shared a bed more than once before this, at various sleepovers.

Why did I have to start falling for her? And even worse, why did I have to fall for her right before we left on a road trip together that would leave us in close quarters for three weeks straight?

Luckily, Bree kept close to her edge of the bed as well without me having to ask her to. For a moment, just one brief moment, I wondered if she was doing it for the same reason as me. I allowed myself to revel in the fantasy that Bree might actually like me back and was just as scared to say anything. But then I forced myself back into reality, where I knew that wasn't the case. Dwelling on any other idea would only spell later heartbreak.

"Do you want me to turn off the lamp?" Bree asked quietly. "I'm going to be up for a little bit longer but I don't need the light."

"Sure. Thanks." The sooner I went to sleep, the sooner this whole thing would be over. Besides, I was dead on my feet. There was a soft click and our side of the room plunged into darkness.

"Goodnight April," Bree whispered.

"Goodnight Bree," I whispered back.

12

IF I THOUGHT FALLING asleep in the same bed as my crush was bad, waking up in the same bed as her was ten times worse. Mainly because when I woke up, her head was on my chest and there was no way I could move it without waking her up too.

In a moment of (gay) panic, I looked around the room. I didn't want to risk anyone else waking up and witnessing this. Both the second bed and the cot were empty, and the bathroom door was open, which meant that Harlee and Kiara were not in the room. I was a little surprised by this since I never considered either of them morning people, especially not compared to me, but I supposed that they were probably less tired than Bree and me since they slept during a lot more of the drive. I think that was part of the reason they let us take the front seats for the whole trip — it was easier for them to lie down in the back.

Since they were out of the room, it was safe to assume that they were out getting breakfast. Unfortunately, I had no way of knowing when they left or how long they would be gone, so they could walk in and witness the current scene at any moment. To a certain extent, I felt like it shouldn't feel any weirder than me almost lying on top of Bree in the diner the day before. But this was significantly more intimate. For one thing, we were in a bed. For another, there was only a very thin pyjama top between Bree's head and my chest. And, perhaps most notably, there wasn't anyone talking about cannibalism in the background.

And because I had no way of knowing when Kiara and Harlee might get back, I needed to get out of the current predicament as quickly as possible. Preferably without waking up Bree, since that would only serve to embarrass both of us significantly more.

My left arm was hanging freely off the bed. As gently as possible, I used that hand to slowly push Bree's head off of me and back onto the pillow like it had been before. I wasn't sure how she had moved over so far in the night. Luckily, she rolled back easily and I was able to quickly slip out of the bed without her ever being the wiser. I grabbed my clothes and ran into the bathroom, my heart beating wildly in my chest.

Once I made sure the bathroom door was closed and locked, I sighed loudly.

"Why the hell did I go on this trip?" I muttered to myself. I knew it was a bad idea — I should have cancelled it when I had the chance. I was in way over my head.

13

HARLEE AND KIARA were back in the room when I got out of the shower. As expected, they had a Tim Horton's bag and a tray of coffee with them. Their heads were pressed together and they were whispering and giggling about something. I found it a bit odd that they were whispering at a quiet enough volume that I couldn't hear what they were saying at all since they weren't exactly the type to keep secrets, but I assumed they were just trying to keep quiet so as not to wake up Bree.

When I walked over to their side of the room, Harlee hushed Kiara before turning to me.

"There's a bagel BLT in there for you, April," Harlee said. "I got it on a sesame seed bagel. I hope that's all right, I couldn't remember your exact order."

It wasn't my favourite kind of bagel but I wasn't going to complain when she went out of her way to get it for me.

"Yeah, that's good Harlee. Thanks," I said. She smiled and nodded once. I grabbed the bagel and sat down on the desk chair since that was the only available space that wasn't the floor or the bed Bree was sleeping on. Harlee and Kiara went back to whispering to each other, so I pulled out my phone and scrolled through Instagram for entertainment until Bree woke up. About fifteen minutes later, she finally began to stir.

"Morning," Bree said, rubbing her eyes.

"Morning, sleepy-head," Kiara said.

"What time is it?" Bree asked.

"Only nine-thirty," Kiara said. "But we've all been awake for a while."

"Oh," Bree said. "Sorry you had to wait for me. You could have woken me up."

Kiara shrugged. "It's no problem. We've just been hanging out."

Bree got up and went into the bathroom to get ready. While she did that, the three of us finished packing the rest of our things and left our bags by the doors. Bree got ready quickly then did the same, so we were all good to go by ten o'clock.

"We have food for you here, Bree," Harlee said. "Do you want to eat before we leave?"

"Oh yeah, that would be great," she said. She began walking over there but paused when she passed me.

"Something wrong?" I asked.

"Your shirt tag is sticking out. I'll get it," she said. Her cool hands brushed my back as she tucked it in for me. Time slowed around us. Shivers ran down my spine. Her mouth was right by my ear as she softly said, "There you go."

Then she pulled away again, and it was all over.

"Thanks," I said. I stepped back, desperately needing

to put some space between us, and sat on the end of the bed.

Kiara and Harlee were whispering to each other again and soon began laughing loudly. I ignored them and began scrolling on my phone again.

"What are you guys laughing about over there?" Bree asked. She had always been more curious than me. Harlee and Kiara glanced at each other. A silent conversation passed between them before Kiara held her phone up to Bree. Not wanting to be the only one who didn't know what was going on, I moved closer to see what it was as well.

I almost instantly regretted that decision when I was confronted with an image of Bree and me cuddling in our sleep.

"Oh," Bree said. Kiara dissolved into a fit of laughter again, while Harlee giggled. Bree looked back at me. "Well, that's not a big deal. Girls cuddle all the time."

Despite her words, her face was turning bright red. It was always easy to see when Bree was embarrassed since she blushed so easily. This made Harlee and Kiara laugh even harder.

"Yeah, it's normal," I said, hoping my tone came off as casual. I really wanted to curl up and die, but I wasn't about to let them know that.

"Sure it's normal, but it's weird for you two to do it," Kiara said in between her giggles.

"What's that supposed to mean?" Bree asked in a hurt voice. My heart sunk in my chest. They knew. At the very least, Kiara and Harlee knew how I felt about Bree. What else could that comment mean?

Harlee locked eyes with me. I subtly shook my head,

hoping that she would know what I meant. Luckily, Bree was facing them and not me, so she didn't notice. The smile slowly fell off Harlee's face.

"She just meant because you're both gay," Harlee said quickly. Kiara frowned and opened her mouth but Harlee hit her arm lightly. Through gritted teeth, she said, "Right, Kiara?"

Kiara looked at her in confusion. When Bree glanced the other way, Harlee subtly nodded towards me. Kiara's mouth opened in 'o.'

"Right," Kiara said. She nodded her head quickly. "That's exactly what I meant."

Bree still looked a little confused — probably because our entire friend group is gay and she didn't understand why Kiara and Harlee thought it was particularly funny that it was Bree and I cuddling — but she didn't question them further.

Kiara and Harlee began whispering to each other again. Although I couldn't hear them, I knew they were continuing their previous conversation and therefore whispering about me, which grated more than a little. My hand clenched in a fist. I wanted to snap at them to shut up, perhaps ask them how they would feel if somebody whispered about them like that, but I took a deep breath and forced myself to turn away.

Once I had calmed down enough, I asked, "Should we get going?"

They wouldn't be able to talk without us hearing in the car and I was anxious to get on the road, so leaving would be a win-win.

They readily agreed and we headed out.

"We don't have any big plans for the day yet, do we?" Kiara asked once we were in the car.

"I don't think so," I said. I pulled out of the parking space. "Why?"

"I was thinking that we should dye your hair this afternoon," she said. "That's something you wanted to do, isn't it?"

I smiled. "It is indeed. Let's do it."

❧ 14 ❧

DESPITE GETTING A good night's rest, Harlee, Bree and Kiara all fell asleep within thirty minutes of us leaving the hotel. I didn't mind driving in silence, but it was a stark difference to the past couple of days, when I'd never had a moment alone.

I stopped to get gas about an hour into the trip. A minute after I had gotten out of the car, the backseat door on the far side opened up and Harlee climbed out. She closed the door quietly behind her so as not to wake up Bree and Kiara then walked around the back of the car to where I was standing, pumping gas.

"Hey," I said. "I thought you were asleep."

"I woke up when the car stopped," Harlee explained. She stretched her arms up overhead and yawned. "Figured I should take the chance to stretch my legs."

"Yeah, that's a good plan," I said. Harlee pulled up the sleeves of her loose knit cardigan. I was absolutely certain she was wearing it as a fashion statement since the day was not nearly warm enough to have almost bare arms. The heat wave that we'd been experiencing the week before was definitely over. Harlee was like that; she always put in a lot of effort into the clothes she wore, then made them look like they were entirely effortless, and half the time, she wasn't even dressed for the right season.

"So," Harlee said, with a glance around. "Any idea where we are?"

"Not a clue," I said. We were well into Ontario by that point. I'd been following the directions on her GPS so I knew we were headed in the right direction, but the drive was definitely going to be full of stopping in random small towns none of us had ever heard of.

"I'm glad you and Bree thought of this," Harlee said. She stuck her hands in the back pockets of her jeans. "It's going to be really fun."

I forced a small smile and looked down, unsure exactly how to respond. Out of the four of us, I had always been the worst at expressing emotion. I cleared my throat.

"Yeah. I'm looking forward to it."

We stood in an uncomfortable silence for a couple of moments. Harlee and I were pretty similar people in many respects but I sometimes found that conversations didn't flow naturally when it was just the two of us alone.

"So, do you think we should keep using the same sleeping situation that we did last night?" Harlee asked. My heart thudded in my chest at the mention of the night before. "I mean, I know we won't usually have a cot there too, but like Kiara mentioned, she's the only one who can stand my kicking."

I narrowed my eyes at the mischievous look on her

face. I thought we had some sort of understanding that morning when she stopped Kiara from teasing Bree and I about the photo, but now I was questioning that.

"I don't know," I said. I did not want to have that conversation right then. "I guess we'll have to talk about it tonight."

Harlee nodded. I prayed that would be the end of the conversation, but I knew it wouldn't be as soon as I heard Harlee open her mouth again.

"Hey, one of the things on your list was to fall in love, wasn't it?" She asked. I internally sighed and glanced at the gas meter. There was still a little ways to go. There was no way of getting out of this.

"It was," I said slowly. Harlee glanced in the car then looked back at me with a big grin.

"Well, Bree's right there," she said. "What are you waiting for?"

My stomach dropped. The smile on Harlee's face suddenly seemed sinister rather than sweet or just mischievous. There were a few ways I could play this situation, and I had mere seconds to choose which way I was going to do it. Harlee probably wanted me to admit my crush so she could help me act on it, but there was no chance in hell that was happening.

I laughed in a way that I hoped was believable but sounded fake to my own ears.

"Right," I said. "As if Bree and I would ever work."

Harlee shrugged, the grin still ever-present on her face. "Opposites attract, babe."

I shook my head so much that it hurt a little. I told myself I was only arguing so much because I didn't want to even suspect that there might be something there, but really, I think I was trying to convince myself. If I told myself enough times that Bree and I would never work, then the crush would just disappear again and we could all go back to normal.

"Not us," I insisted. "We're too different."

Harlee shrugged again, in a *whatever you say, but we both know I'm right* kind of way.

"I'm going to get a chocolate bar from the gas station," she said. "You want anything?"

I shook my head mutely. I was suddenly feeling a little sick. Harlee nodded. As she walked off, I got a gnawing feeling in my chest that there was something I meant to get from the store, although I had no idea what it was. When she was halfway across the parking lot, I remembered that Bree had mentioned to me earlier that she wanted snacks. For a moment, I considered not mentioning it. But it wasn't fair to Bree for me to do that, just to save myself a little bit of embarrassment.

"Harlee!" I called. Harlee glanced back, her hand on the metal door handle of the shop. I had a moment of panic where I realized Bree hadn't mentioned exactly what she wanted, just that she wanted snacks in general. I took a gamble and named some stuff I knew she liked. "Can you get Bree some salt and vinegar potato chips and a vitamin water?"

"What flavour water?"

"Uh... the pink one." Hell if I knew what any of the flavours were. The only time I'd ever been within a five foot radius of a bottle of vitamin water was when I was around Bree. It was her favourite drink of all time. "And wipe that smirk off your face."

Harlee did not wipe the smirk off her face, but it

didn't matter anyway because she turned around to walk inside. I tried to focus on paying for the gas, but the entire time, all I could think about was how happy Bree would be when she woke up and found out that we had bought the snacks for her. I slammed my hand against the stone pillar beside me and wondered when I had gotten so soft. I had no doubt that it was sometime around when I had met Bree.

☙ 15 ❧

Bree and I went to the drug store that afternoon to buy hair dye. Her hands were full when we got back to the room so she tried to open the door with her foot, which went about as well as I would have anticipated.

"I can just open the door," I said. I reached out to do so with my free hand, but Bree quickly kicked it away.

"No!" She said in a determined voice. "I've got this."

I rolled her eyes and pointedly ignored the way my heart melted at the sight of Bree desperately trying to push the door handle down. I had never noticed before, but Bree tended to stick out her tongue when she was trying to concentrate on something, and for some reason, that made my heart pound a little bit faster than usual.

Not because I had a crush on Bree, mind you.

I brushed off my pounding heart and warm face as being because of the walk from the car, even though we had only taken about twenty steps. Meanwhile, Bree finally managed to get enough of a grip on the door with her foot. I wasn't sure how it was physically possible with her hard-soled shoe on but I chose not to question it at that moment, as she slowly pushed the door inward. Once it had swung far enough in, Bree dropped her foot, caught the door with her shoulder, and walked into the room, with me following behind her. We dropped everything on the closest bed.

"Looks like Harlee and Kiara laid out the tarps already," Bree said, nodding toward the bathroom. I looked over. The floor was covered in cut up trash bags that were taped together so that any dye that inevitably fell on the floor wouldn't stain the tile.

"I wonder where they went," I said. I'd assumed they would be in the room when we got back but that clearly wasn't the case.

"Probably just outside. Harlee said something about sitting by the pond earlier. I'll go get them."

"Oh, you don't need to do that," I said. There wasn't any big rush to get anything done. I sat down on the bed and sighed in contentment. The mattress was a little too hard and the comforter was a strange texture, but there was a perfect sunbeam hitting the exact spot where I was sitting, and all I wanted to do was stretch out and take a nap. "This can wait a little. They might as well enjoy the sun while it's still out."

Bree nodded and sat down on the other bed.

"What about you?" She asked.

"Hm?" I laid down on my back. Bree mimicked the action.

"Don't you want to go out and enjoy the sun while it's still out?"

I shrugged. "You know, I would but I'm comfortable here. How about you?"

Bree laughed. "Same."

We fell into a comfortable silence. A rare smile donned my face. I couldn't quite explain the feeling that I had in my chest, a sort of warm and fuzzy feeling that made me unable to resist the smile. It was a feeling I hadn't had in a long time. There was just something about lying in that room with Bree, even if we were on separate beds, even if we were in complete silence, that made me feel whole.

I wished the feeling would never end.

16

"ALL RIGHT, LET'S DO THIS," Kiara said. She snapped the second glove on then reached for the hair dye. Though I was not generally a nervous person, I watched her warily in the mirror. I was concerned at the level of confidence Kiara seemed to have in her non-existent abilities surrounding cosmetology.

"You watched a video on how to do this, right?" I asked for the third time that day.

"Will you relax?" Kiara asked. She shook the bottle of dye then squeezed it out in the small plastic bowl. I cringed as I looked at the black liquid that would soon be put on my hair. Though I had wanted to dye my hair black for many years, I was suddenly having second thoughts. "What's the worst that can happen?"

"It could look terrible," Harlee supplied. "And black is an awful colour to try and get out again."

At least Harlee was honest.

Kiara rolled her eyes. "Don't worry, April, it's going to

look great. And it's not like we're bleaching it, so we can't absolutely destroy your hair."

"I don't think she would let us bleach her hair," Bree said. She made eye contact with me in the mirror and grinned wryly.

I would let you do anything.

Kiara scooped a glob of hair dye out of the bowl and unceremoniously dropped it on my scalp. I cringed at the cold sensation, and cringed even more, if that was possible, when Kiara began dragging her gloved fingers through my hair to spread out the dye.

"You did watch the video, right?" I asked again. I was realizing that Kiara had never actually given me a straight answer to the question, despite the number of times I'd asked.

Kiara's movements faltered. "Yeah. Sure."

"You do not sound certain of that." My hands tightly gripped the arms of the chair I was sitting in. My entire body tensed like I was going to get up and walk away, which was all I wanted to do, but I was in far too deep now to do anything but suffer through this. Who knew how my hair would look if I tried just washing out the dye she'd already placed.

"Like I said," Kiara said, dropping another handful of dye on my scalp, "you need to trust me."

"How am I supposed to trust you when you clearly have *no idea what you're doing?*" My voice was nearing a yell as I watched the black dye get unevenly smeared all over my hair. Even the ever-optimistic Bree was cringing at that point.

"It will be fine," Kiara insisted again. "Just enjoy the process."

I suddenly regretted every decision I had made in my life that led me to this.

17

My hair didn't turn out as bad as I expected. Granted, that wasn't saying much, but it was something.

I couldn't stop looking at it. After we finished our dinner that night and were waiting for the cheque, I looked at myself in my phone camera again. The dye job wasn't great, but I was still obsessed with the look. I had wanted dark hair for years but my parents would never let me dye it, so it felt surreal to finally have it.

Kiara leaned forward on the table, looking immensely proud of herself.

"What do you think of it, April?" She asked. "Did we do a good job?"

I stared at her for a moment too long. I didn't know how to say that it wasn't very good without hurting her feelings, even if I didn't mind that it looked like a DIY job.

"Uh-huh," I said finally. They all laughed.

Bree brushed her hand through my hair and I froze. From her point of view, I'm sure she viewed it as a completely normal thing to do, given how touchy-feely our friend group was. But when she ran her hand through my hair like that, when she smiled at me in a way that I felt was reserved for me and said that she thought it looked great, it made me forget how to breathe.

How was there ever a time that I wasn't hopelessly in love with her?

"You two are a cute couple," somebody said. "How long have you been together?"

They were talking to somebody else, I was sure. Why would somebody ask if Bree and I were a couple? That would be something out of a dream for me.

Except then Bree looked up at the person behind me, smiled sweetly, and said, "Oh, we've been together for a few months now."

Wait, what? Am I dreaming?

The person behind me, I assumed it was our waitress due to the receipt that was now lying on the table, responded but I didn't hear the words at all. I felt like I was underwater, unable to make sense of the garbled sounds around me. Bree's hand was no longer in my hair, but it was on my shoulder and she was leaning into me, like we were a couple, like we were talking to somebody as a couple. My pulse sped up so fast that I didn't know how anybody else couldn't hear it. I stared at her in awe, at her beautiful pink lips that were covered in lipgloss and pulled into a beautiful smile, at the way her eyes lit up as she spoke, and her blonde hair fell around her shoulders.

Then the dam broke again. She pulled away. I looked behind me but there wasn't anybody there anymore. Harlee and Kiara were laughing. Were they laughing at me or someone else? Had somebody said something funny?

What the hell is happening?

"Thanks for going along with that, April," Bree said. She was staring at me again. Expecting me to do something again. *When in doubt, smile and nod.* "I just didn't want to embarrass her."

"I never took you as someone who's good at lying, Bree," Kiara said. "Especially on the spot like that."

Bree shrugged. "It was barely a lie. That is really how we met. I just... embellished it a little."

Harlee shook her head and smiled. "We can never visit this town again, either."

Bree laughed. "At this rate, we'll never be able to leave our hometowns again."

"Bold of you to assume I'm not embarrassed to be seen around my hometown too," Kiara said.

The three of them kept laughing and joking. I stopped trying to keep up. Instead, I just leaned back in my chair, stayed quiet, and wished that everything Bree told that waitress hadn't been a lie.

❧ 18 ❧

WE HAD OUR LONGEST drive thus far the next day. On most days, we drove a maximum of four hours, oftentimes less. But that day, we were about six and a half hours out from Elyssa's house, and it seemed like a waste to stop in the middle of that drive when we all really wanted to get to the house as soon as possible so we decided to power through it. We all pretended that the only reason we wanted to get there so badly was to see Elyssa — and that was a large part of it — but it was definitely also because we wanted to sleep in comfortable beds, take showers with good water pressure, and have home-cooked meals. We hadn't been on the road for long but there was no denying that we all missed the comforts of being home.

Bree and I decided to split the drive into three two-hour sections, rather than in two sections like we usually did. As usual, Harlee and Kiara slept for the first portion of the drive. I glanced at them in the rearview mirror every once in a while. They had a couple of pillows stacked in the middle seat, and were both laying on them as much as possible, while still wearing their seatbelts. For a while, I thought Bree was asleep too since she was being so quiet but when I looked over at her, she was resting her chin on her hand and staring out the window.

"Enjoying the scenery?" I asked. It took her a couple of moments to register that I was talking to her and look over. I felt a twinge of guilt for distracting her.

"Yeah," she said, with a grin. "I was just thinking about how peaceful it is out here. It's nice to be away from the city, don't you think?"

"Yeah, it is," I agreed readily. Not that I was in the city all that much during the summer, anyway, given where I lived. Come to think of it, I wasn't sure what Bree's hometown was like at all. I knew the general whereabouts and that it was on the smaller side, but beyond that, it could have been any old town. "Hey, I just realized I don't know anything about where you're from."

"Oh," Bree said. She didn't say anything else, though, which led to an uncomfortable silence. I looked at her from the corner of my eye. I could almost see the gears turning in her head, as though she was trying to figure out how on earth the two of us had been friends for eight months without the topic ever coming up. To be honest, I was wondering the same thing. I knew plenty of stories from Bree's life, but none of them told me anything about where she was from.

Since it seemed like Bree wasn't going to answer, I decided to keep the conversation going.

"I'm from a small town, myself," I said. "Pretty out in the middle of nowhere."

That broke Bree out of whatever trance she had been in. "Did you like it there?"

"It was all right," I said. I hadn't brought up the topic so talk about myself, so I tried to spin it back to her. "So, where are you from?"

"Oh, I'm from Vancouver originally, but my family moved to Stephenville, Manitoba in my senior year."

"Sounds like a fun transition," I said. I changed lanes.

"It wasn't the best timing, that's for sure," Bree said. "I was pretty annoyed with it at first, but now I don't care so much."

"Would you have considered going to university out here if your family hadn't moved?" I asked.

"No way," she said firmly. "My plan was always to only apply to schools on the west coast. But then we left and," she paused, "I don't know, I didn't really want to go back."

"You would have missed your family too much?"

"Yeah, I guess," she muttered. She played with the bracelet on her wrist. "I think there was also something special about coming here and having nobody know about my past. I could be whoever I wanted."

"Do you have a secret criminal history I don't know about or something?"

She laughed. "Do I look like a criminal to you?"

"No, but it's always the ones you least suspect."

She laughed again and I grinned to myself.

"I was thinking more along the lines of my transition," Bree said in a more serious voice. "I mean, I'm proud to be trans but sometimes, it's nice to not have to worry about how somebody might react to it, you know? When I still lived in the town I grew up in, everyone knew and everyone had an opinion. This way, I get to decide who knows and who doesn't."

I nodded slowly. "People underestimate the power of that."

"Yeah, they really do." She looked out the window again, sinking deep into her thoughts. I thought that would be the end of the conversation, but a minute later, she turned towards me again. "Did you ever consider going far away for school?"

"Yeah, I did," I said. I considered how much I wanted to share with her. As a whole, I wasn't a very open person, but Bree had just opened up to me and I wanted to reciprocate. "For a while, I really wanted to get away from everyone I knew, and just start a new life."

She tilted her head. "But you didn't in the end?"

I sighed and stared straight ahead at the road, but I could feel Bree's curious eyes burning a hole in the side of her head.

"The main reason I thought I wanted to get away was because I didn't want to be near my ex-girlfriend," I said. "We broke up at the beginning of grade twelve, just before we did university applications so I had my heart set on going as far as possible. But once some time passed and I could think about it critically, I decided I didn't want to go quite so far after all."

"Why not?"

I sighed. "I decided I didn't want to let her rule my life, especially when she wasn't a part of it anymore."

"That's really smart," Bree said softly. I shrugged. We went back to riding in silence.

❧ 19 ❦

AFTER WE SWITCHED DRIVERS, I pulled the list out of my bag. We hadn't really been keeping track of what we had already completed and what we still had left to do, and I was worried that we might miss something. I grabbed a pencil and began putting a checkmark next to the things I had finished, whether it was in the past few years or on this trip: *get a tattoo, go on a road trip, hike a mountain, learn how to drive, dance in the rain, swim in the ocean, dye my hair, read 100 books in one year, learn a second language* (I don't even know why I included that on the list — by the time I wrote this list, I had already been learning French for years at school), *run a 10K, learn how to play an instrument, graduate high school, donate blood,* and *be out and proud.* Now that I could see what was finished and what wasn't, the list looked a lot less overwhelming.

I ran my finger over number eleven: *fall in love — real love.* I surreptitiously glanced at Bree, then back down at the list. I was not going to fall in love with her. That much I had promised myself. Not wanting a repeat of the conversation I'd had with Harlee the other day at the gas station, I went ahead and checked it off. If anyone asked, I would just tell them that I counted my ex-girlfriend, Tina, as falling in "real love".

"How much is there left?" Bree asked.

"Hm?"

"On the list. How many items are left?"

"Oh, uh, only five," I said after quickly counting. "Go skinny dipping, camp in Algonquin, watch the sunrise, conquer a fear, and make a new list."

"That's not bad!" She said. "Three-quarters of the way through."

"Yeah," I said. I tucked the list back into my bag. "I should definitely be able to finish on time."

I didn't mention that it wouldn't be real. I knew in my heart that I didn't count Tina as someone I truly fell in love with. But I didn't want them to feel like they had done all this to help me, only to fail because of one item.

"Oh, for sure!" Bree said. She tapped her hands against the steering wheel. "Let's see... camp in Algonquin is easy, that's what we're going to do anyway. While we're there, we can watch the sunrise. I guess we could go skinny dipping there, but it might be easier to see if we can do it at Elyssa's cottage."

"You want to go skinny dipping at Elyssa's mother's house?" I asked.

"Well, it sounds weird if you put it like that."

"It sounds weird however you say it."

"Well if you want to finish the list while on this trip, then you either have to go skinny dipping in the lake at Elyssa's house or in a lake in Algonquin Park. Take your pick."

I hated to admit it, but she had a point.

"We can ask her about it later," I conceded.

"Well yeah, I wouldn't recommend showing up at her house and asking immediately. Anyway, onto the other two things. Making a new list is easy—"

"It's not as easy as you would think, actually," I said. "It took me a good few days to come up with everything on that list. And now I've used up a bunch of good ideas."

"But this time, we'll have five people brainstorming instead of one," Bree said. "Either way, we have two weeks to think of stuff. Then the last one... what was the last one again?"

"Conquer a fear," I said.

"Hm... what did you want to do for that one?"

"I hadn't really thought about it." I didn't tell her this, but that was the one I was the most worried about. I hadn't decided what I wanted to do for it since the prompt was so vague, but I knew I didn't want to cheat my way through it.

"Right," Bree said. She chewed on her lip as she thought for a moment. "You're scared of heights, right?"

"What?" I asked. I didn't remember ever telling her that. "How did you know that?"

"You mentioned it when we went on that hike last year," she said. "You didn't want to stand too close to the edge because you were scared of heights."

"Oh. Right." I wasn't sure how I felt about her knowing that. Obviously, I knew that a fear of heights was entirely common and nothing to be embarrassed about, but all the same, I didn't love people knowing my weaknesses. Even someone as sweet as Bree.

"Have you ever been cliff jumping?" She asked.

"Cliff jumping?" I didn't follow her train of thought."

"Yeah. Elyssa mentioned that there's somewhere on the lake where she likes to go. That would be conquering your fear of heights."

"Oh, um, I don't know..." Cliff jumping would definitely count as conquering a fear, but I wasn't sure if I wanted to do it. There were a lot of risks involved, and I thought that maybe it would be easier if I conquered a different fear — but the only other fear I could think of was admitting my feelings to Bree.

"Come on, April!" She said. "You can do it!"

"Cliff jumping can be dangerous, Bree." I could just see myself jumping in the wrong spot and getting seriously injured. I was surprised she was so into the idea, given how cautious she usually was.

"It can also be very fun. We can do it together." She glanced at me then looked back at the road again. With a mischievous grin, she said, "I can even hold your hand."

I forced myself to laugh with her. I forced myself not to say that I would love it. Because there was no way I could convincingly make that sound like a joke.

"Fine," I said before I could talk myself out of it.

"Really?" She asked excitedly.

I nodded. "Sure. Have to do something, right?"

I didn't say what I was really thinking: *I would do anything as long as you're there with me.*

20

A COUPLE OF HOURS LATER, the four of us walked into the small grocery store. We were originally just stopping to switch drivers, but then Harlee pointed out how rude it is to show up at somebody's house empty-handed, so we decided to get Elyssa's mother some wine and flowers as a thank you for letting us stay.

"All right, I told Elyssa we'll be there in two or three hours," Bree said, slipping her phone into her pocket.

"Perfect," I replied.

"Here's the wine aisle," Harlee said. She paused in front of the selection. "Although, now that I'm thinking about it, we would have better luck at an actual alcohol store."

"Alcohol store?" Kiara asked in amusement.

"I don't know what stores they have in Ontario!" Harlee said.

"They have the LCBO," Bree supplied. She pulled up Google Maps. "But there isn't one anywhere near here, so unless we want to go out of our way a little..."

"This will be fine," Harlee said. She grabbed a bottle of red wine off the shelf. "This looks nice enough. Now onto flowers."

She led the way out of the aisle again, not giving us a chance to argue. To be fair, she definitely knew the most about wine, and I was sure the rest of us did not have any strong opinions on the matter anyway.

The flowers were at the front of the shop. There wasn't a very big selection, but there was still enough for us to argue over which ones we should pick.

"How about this one?" Kiara asked. "A calla lily."

"No," Bree said immediately.

"Why not?" Kiara asked.

"You know why."

"What's wrong with it?" I asked. My view was blocked by some other plants.

"It's inappropriate," Bree said.

"How can a flower be inappropriate?" I asked.

"It looks like a pussy," Harlee supplied. She grabbed the flower from Kiara and held it up so I could see. I blinked. While not an exact replica by any means, I definitely understood what she meant.

"Yeah, we cannot get that for Elyssa's mother," I agreed.

"Why not?" Kiara asked. "We're all gay women, it works out."

"Her mother's not!" I said.

"Technically we don't know that," Kiara said. "Besides, she probably won't even notice."

"Then why do you want to do it so badly?" Bree asked.

Kiara grinned. "Mainly because it would embarrass the hell out of Elyssa."

"No way," I said. I shook my head. "I am not giving that to our host."

"Agreed," Bree said. Kiara rolled her eyes but she put it away.

"You guys have no sense of humour," she said.

"We're not saying her reaction wouldn't be hilarious," Bree said, "because it would be. We just don't want to see her mother's reaction."

"Even if she did notice, she probably wouldn't say anything," Kiara said.

"Let's not test the theory," I said. I grabbed a bouquet of wildflowers. "How about this? Nice, simple and does not resemble genitalia in any way."

"Perfect," Harlee said. "Let's go before we spot something else we like and spend too much money."

We made it halfway to the cash register before Kiara gasped loudly and ran to the other end of the store.

"I think you jinxed it, Harlee," I said dryly. She glared at me as we followed Kiara.

"Pride pins!" Kiara called excitedly. She was standing in front of two bins, each of them filled with a bunch of small pins. Kiara was standing in front of the one closest to us, so I went to the other one. The first thing I noticed was the collection of lesbian flag pins in the pile. I grabbed three of them and handed one to Bree and Harlee respectively.

"Oh, is there a bi one?" Kiara asked.

"I can do you one better," I said. I grabbed the bisexual one and the grey-asexual one and dropped them into her hand. "They have both."

"Sweet!" Kiara said.

"Oh, they have gender flag pins over here," Bree said. She grabbed the transgender one.

"Is there a demi-girl one for Elyssa?" Harlee asked. She peered into the bin as well.

"I don't see it..." Bree said slowly. She moved the pins around. "Oh, never mind, I found one! Should we get it?"

"Yeah, she'll love it," Kiara said. "We should grab her a pansexual one too."

There were a bunch of them littering the top of the pile so I grabbed one.

"Perfect," Harlee said. "We got what we came in for and extra stuff, just like always."

"They're gay pins, Harlee," Kiara said seriously. "We had no choice."

Bree laughed. "There's no arguing with that logic."

21

As we drove the final stretch to Elyssa's cottage, I came to regret my offer to drive us there. On paper, the drive seemed easy enough — mostly sticking to the highways, then about thirty minutes of driving through the countryside. When I looked at the map, I thought the directions looked pretty easy to follow.

If only I knew that half the roads listed on the map were inaccessible, and the three other people in my car had no idea how to navigate.

"I think we have to turn left at the next street," Bree said. She had the paper map spread out over the dashboard.

"Are you sure?" I asked. I had taken more than one wrong turn already.

She bit her lip. "No, not really."

I sighed. That was how the whole trip had been going so far.

"How about you, Harlee?" I asked. Harlee had Google Maps open on her phone and was also trying to navigate. I hoped that with the two of them giving directions, we might end up actually going the right way. "Where do you think I should turn?"

"Uh, I think it's a right," Harlee said. "But not at the next street, it's the one after."

"That's the exact opposite of what Bree just told me to do." I glanced at her in the rearview mirror, only to be met with a helpless shrug.

"Elyssa said that you're supposed to turn left at the moose statue," Kiara said. In addition to the paper map and electronic map, we also had Elyssa's directions that involved landmarks as our guide instead of street names.

"At the what?" I asked. Thank goodness that the street was going on forever without anywhere to turn.

"All it says is moose statue," Kiara said. "I don't know what to tell you."

"All right," I said. "Everyone be on the lookout for a moose statue, then."

We drove for long enough that I thought my assumption about the moose statue not being real was correct, but eventually, Bree yelled, "Moose!" She yelled it right in my ear so it was a little loud and I jerked the steering wheel in shock, but I appreciated the enthusiasm.

Once I turned onto the street, I asked them where we were supposed to go next. Bree was turning the paper map every which way like she wasn't even sure which direction we were going. Harlee said she had lost her cell connection so she couldn't guide us using Google Maps anymore.

"Well, that's great," I muttered.

"Let's just follow Elyssa's directions," Harlee said.

"They're weird but they're easier to follow than these maps."

I didn't really care what we did at that point, as long as someone told me where to go.

"Fine," I said. "What's the next instruction?"

"Turn left at the giant rock," Kiara said.

"What?" I asked through gritted teeth.

"What?" Kiara asked innocently. "That seems easy enough."

"Kiara," I said slowly, "in case you haven't noticed, *we're surrounded by giant rocks!*"

Bree placed her hand gently on my arm.

"Why don't we switch?" She suggested in a soft voice. A placating voice. "I know you get frustrated with bad directions."

"There's a gas station coming up," Harlee said, pointing ahead. I could just see it in the distance. "Why don't you switch there?"

I didn't really want to switch. I just wanted to arrive at the cottage already and relax. But Bree looked very concerned about me and I hated to make her feel concerned, so I decided to go along with it.

When I got out of the car, Bree pulled me aside for a second.

"What are you doing, Bree?" I asked, agitated. "We have to keep going."

"We can stand to wait a minute," she said. She put her hands on my arms. "Are you all right?"

"Why wouldn't I be?"

She shrugged. "You seem upset about something. I just wanted to see if I could help at all."

I wanted to snap at her that I was fine and we needed

to stop wasting time worrying about feelings. But I would never snap at Bree, not when she was being so sweet.

"I'm just tired," I said. I grinned ruefully. "And really sick of driving. Who could have guessed that would happen on a road trip, huh?"

She laughed. "Remember, Elyssa said we can stay at her place for a little bit. We don't have a campsite booked in Algonquin for another few days anyway, so we can take some time off from driving before we continue. Truth be told, I'm a little tired of all of this too."

I closed my eyes and took a couple of deep breaths. Then I nodded.

"Yeah," I said. I reopened my eyes. "Yeah, taking a few days off will be good."

Bree smiled. "Come on. I'll drive the rest of the way. Hopefully, we're not too far."

"Who even knows at this point," I said. We climbed back in the car. Harlee and Kiara didn't say anything about how long it took us to get back or make any mention of whether they could hear our conversation, which I was extremely grateful for.

"Let's get this show on the road," Bree said.

"You sound like my dad," Kiara said.

"Hey!"

The rest of the drive went a lot more smoothly, mainly because Bree was at the wheel. The directions were no less confusing, but she found them funny and took them in stride as she drove. I couldn't help but smile at her good outlook on everything.

"That was the tree with weird leaves," Kiara said, about forty-five minutes into the drive. "Which means we're almost there. She said the cottage is... blue-ish with white trim."

We were driving on a road that ran parallel to the lake. Between the street and the lake were cottages that appeared every few acres. Bree slowed down and stared at each one intently as we went by.

"Does that look blue enough to you?" She asked. I looked out the window as well. It was a modest one-story blue-grey cottage.

"I have no idea," I said, slowly shaking my head.

"I think we're looking for a two-story place," Harlee said. "So that's probably not it."

"Right," Bree said. We continued driving along.

"You know, some of these places have house numbers," Kiara said. "Why didn't she just give us the number?"

Bree shook her head. "Everything works differently in the country. You can't ask too many questions."

The next three houses could not even be mistaken for the colour blue. We were nearing the end of the street, and getting a little desperate.

"Maybe it was that one-story house," Kiara said.

"Maybe we have the wrong street," Harlee said dryly.

"Or maybe," Bree said. She paused, either for dramatic effect or to get a better look at the cottage at the end of the lane, "It's the house up here!"

She turned onto the long gravel driveway and parked beside the house. It was also a blue-grey colour, but it had the white trim as she had specified and was two stories.

"Hopefully this is the right place," Bree said as we got

out. As if on cue, Elyssa opened the door and came running out to greet us.

"I'm going to go ahead and say that it is," I said.

"You're here!" Elyssa said. "I can't believe you guys are actually here!"

She was dressed in just a bathing suit top and a pair of shorts, and her wavy black hair was loose around her shoulders. She looked so casual and relaxed while the rest of us probably looked like a hot mess.

"Sorry we took so long," I said. "We had some trouble finding the same."

"Right, sorry about that," Elyssa said. "I didn't know how to give better directions than that."

"It's fine!" Bree said. "We made it here didn't we?"

"Let me help you bring your stuff in," Elyssa said. She shook her head. "Oh my gosh, I really can't believe you're here!"

Bree and I smiled at each other. The journey might have been rough but it was worth it to see our friend so happy.

❧ 2 2 ❧

LIKE I'D TOLD Bree in the car, I wasn't planning on asking about skinny dipping the first day we were there. That plan changed when Elyssa's mom left a few hours after we arrived, saying she was going away for the weekend but Elyssa could call her if we had any trouble.

"She's really just leaving us here alone for the weekend?" Bree asked Elyssa.

"Yeah," Elyssa said with a shrug. "I mean, think about it: how much trouble could we really get up to? We're out in the middle of nowhere."

That seemed like as good a time as any to bring up our plan.

"I'm glad to hear you say that, Elyssa," I said.

"Oh, no," she muttered.

"Don't worry, it's nothing too bad," I said. She looked at me dubiously. "I was just wondering if you guys want to go skinny dipping in the lake."

"Skinny dipping?" Elyssa asked. I nodded. "Okay, I

guess that's not too bad... I'm not sure I really want to do that, but you guys are all more than welcome to."

I looked to Kiara and Harlee. "Either of you want to?"

"I'm a little tired," Kiara said. "I don't feel like swimming."

"Don't you think it's going to be really cold?" Harlee asked.

"I guess it will be a little cold," I shrugged. "But we want to do it on this trip and it's not going to get any warmer, so we might as well do it today."

Harlee nodded. "That makes sense. I don't think I want to anyway, though."

I looked to Bree. "Guess it's just you and me. Assuming you still want to, of course."

Bree nodded. "Sure."

"Why don't you two go ahead and do it now?" Elyssa suggested. "Might as well go before it gets pitch black. Kiara, Harlee and I can hang around up here. I'll make dinner."

"Are you sure?" Bree asked. "I don't want to put you out. We can help make dinner first."

Elyssa waved her off. "It's no worries. I'll make dinner while you two go swimming. It will be cold when you get back."

Bree glanced at me, silently asking what I thought of the plan. Honestly, I felt bad too but I knew Elyssa would feel bad if we didn't go. She would think that it was her fault because she hadn't wanted to come.

"We'll do the dishes," I promised. Elyssa nodded, although I wasn't sure whether she was just saying yes for now to get us to stop arguing. Either way, it seemed to appease Bree.

"There are towels in the front closet," Elyssa said. I grabbed two and handed one to Bree.

Bree paused in the doorway and turned back. "But we're not wearing our bathing suits."

It took a few seconds of all of us staring at her blankly for her to realize the mistake. She laughed and shook her head, then turned back around and walked outside.

"Have fun!" Kiara called after us. The evening air was a bit on the colder side, and I started to regret our decision as we ran down the wooden steps.

When we got to the dock, we kicked off our shoes and left our towels with them.

"Are you sure you want to do this?" Bree asked. Her arms were crossed over her chest, and I couldn't tell if it was because it was cold or a sign that she wanted to stay covered up. Or perhaps both. I looked back up at the cottage. The view from the windows was completely obstructed by the trees so the three others wouldn't be able to see us. I found it funny that that reassured me, considering I had wanted them to come in the first place. I guess there was just something different about all of us seeing each other, as compared to them seeing us skinny dipping while sitting fully clothed in the warm cottage.

"I'll regret it if I don't," I said honestly. There was still that same voice in the back of my mind telling me that I already cheated on the *fall in love* part of the list, so I could cheat on this and no one would have to know. But I knew if I did that, then I would just be cheating myself.

"Right," Bree said. She looked at the still water then back at me. She was obviously having cold feet about the whole idea.

"You don't have to do it with me if you don't want to," I said. "I won't hold it against you."

Bree shook her head. "I want to. I really do. I just..."

The silence hung between us.

"You don't have to explain," I said. I got the sense that there was a personal reason she didn't want to do this and I didn't want to push her to explain if she didn't want to.

She stared me in the eyes. "Nobody's ever really seen me naked before, April. Especially not since my transition."

"Okay," I said neutrally. I wasn't exactly sure where she was going with this and I didn't want to make her uncomfortable. I considered reassuring her again that she didn't have to do this with me but I opted to stay silent. She was clearly working up the courage to say something and I didn't want to steer the conversation in a way that she didn't want, or make her feel like she didn't have the space to say how she felt.

"Just promise me you won't laugh," she whispered. I felt a little offended that she thought I would ever laugh at her body, but I reminded myself that she was quite possibly asking this based on prior experience and it wasn't about me.

"I promise," I said.

She nodded. She pulled at the hem of her shirt like she was going to take it off then dropped her arms again.

"Maybe..." she bit her lip. "Maybe we shouldn't look."

"What do you mean?" I asked.

"Like, I'll look away while you take off your clothes," she said. "Then you can jump in and I won't see you. Then you turn away until I'm in the water too."

That was probably for the best for both of us. I nodded. She slowly turned around so she was facing the boathouse instead of me. As quickly as possible, I ripped off my shirt and shorts. I was a little more hesitant when taking off my bra and underwear. It was the most naked I had ever been outside before and it felt... illegal. Which, I suppose, it technically was.

A gust of wind blew across just after I finished taking off my underwear, making me shiver uncontrollably. I was beginning to seriously regret my decision but I was determined to see it through. Before I could talk myself out of it, I jumped off the dock and into the water below.

The first thing I noticed was how distinctly cold the water was. Not just cold but freezing. If there was ever a time not to go skinny dipping, it was that day. What the hell had I been thinking? It was the middle of May — of course, the water was cold. Normally when I went swimming, I used pretty leisurely movements to keep myself afloat, but this time, I kicked extra hard just for the sake of keeping myself warm. As an added side benefit, it kept my mind off the fact that I was bare naked in a lake.

"Can I turn around now?" Bree asked.

"Yeah," I said. She turned. Goosebumps raised on my arms as she looked at me.

"How's the water?" She asked. "Is it very cold?"

I considered telling her the truth but I was pretty sure if I did that then she wouldn't jump in.

"No, it's really comfortable," I said. She looked at me

apprehensively. My teeth chattering as I spoke probably didn't help my case.

"If you say so," she said.

Remembering my end of the deal, I turned around so she could get changed. I realized that I hadn't checked whether it was easy to see through the water or not, so for all I knew, she could easily see my body under the water. I tried to push that thought out of my mind. Bree wasn't one to take advantage of a situation like that.

A moment later, she jumped into the water behind me. Some water droplets hit the back of my head and neck. When I heard her resurface, I turned around, and immediately got hit in the face by a spray of water.

"Hey!" I sputtered. I splashed water back at her. "What was that for?"

"You said the water is a comfortable temperature! This is freezing!"

"You wouldn't have jumped in if I told you it was freezing!"

She didn't have a response for that.

"Don't expect me to stay in for long," she said.

I grinned. "Why not put it to the test?"

"What do you mean?"

"Let's see who can stay in the water the longest." Technically, the game wouldn't be fair since I got in first, but I was certain I could stay in longer than her, so I didn't mind.

"I'll take you up on that," she said. Then she splashed water in my face again.

"Hey!"

I did the same back to her and it soon became an all-out water fight. Let me tell you, that's not easy to do in freezing cold water that's too deep to stand it.

"Truce, truce!" Bree called after a minute. I slowly put my hand back down, secretly grateful. I had gotten multiple facefuls of water and I felt as though I was in an ice bath. "How about we just talk instead?"

"You're the one who started the war," I reminded her.

"I know, I know," she sighed. "I didn't think it through."

Suddenly, the sky clouded over, and it began raining on us. Between the cold lake, cold air, and cold raindrops, I was about ready to tap out and run back up the cottage. I was just about to say so and admit defeat when Bree beat me to it.

"That's it!" She said. She swam back to the ladder. "I'm done!"

For a moment, I considered trying to stay in for another minute or two, so it was indisputable that I won but my fingers and toes were starting to go numb.

"Yeah, me too," I said.

She climbed out quickly and I was hot on her heels. She grabbed both our towels, then turned to hand me mine.

And that is when we realized our great mistake.

To her credit, Bree pulled her eyes away quickly, but I knew she had already seen everything. Just like I had seen everything in that split second before I looked down. I quickly grabbed my towel and wrapped it around myself the way I would after a shower and she did the same. I coughed awkwardly, unsure of what to say.

"Well, I think it's safe to say our friendship will never be the same again," she said. She laughed, though it felt forced and awkward. I laughed along, though I'm sure I was no more convincing.

Oh, Bree, you have no idea.

For the whole trip, I'd told myself that my feelings would disappear soon enough and everything would go back to normal. But after that night, I was certain that I was never going to be able to see her as just a friend again.

❦ 23 ❦

"I KNOW IT'S SMALL, but it really is a fun town!" Elyssa said. She parked the truck on the side of the road and we all jumped out. Bree and I made eye contact for just a moment before I broke my gaze and looked toward the shops across the street. "So, what do you guys want to do first?"

"Can we get ice cream?" Kiara asked. She bounced on her toes. "You've mentioned the ice cream shop here so many times, I can't wait to try it."

"Sure," Elyssa said. She started walking, gesturing for us to follow. "It's right down here. The Cheery Creamery."

I snorted at the name. It sounded like the name a five-year-old would choose when playing store, rather than an actual business. I saw Bree grin at me out of the corner of my eye and I wondered if she knew what I was thinking. I was sure she loved the name. Somehow our opposite opinions on things made us fit together in an odd opposites-attract sort of way that I didn't have with many other people.

I had been walking alone at the back of the group, but Bree slowed her steps until she ended up next to me.

"What flavour are you going to get?" She asked.

I just shrugged, making sure to only look forward. I hadn't been able to look at Bree really since seeing her after we got out of the water the night before. When she didn't immediately start talking like she normally would, I felt bad and tried to fill in the conversation.

"Probably something chocolatey," I said.

"That sounds good!" She said. "I'm torn between something really sweet, or something more fruity."

"Why not both?" I asked. "Chocolate and raspberry go well together."

Although I wasn't looking directly at her, I could still see her face from my peripheral vision. Her eyes widened in amazement like I had just shown her the secrets of the universe.

"I never even thought of that," she said. Despite everything going on, I laughed.

"Here we are!" Elyssa said. She held open the door to the shop so that we could walk in.

The shop was small and quaint. On the far wall, there was a counter with a cash register and the ice creams on display. On the right wall, there was a huge menu that listed ice cream flavours, cone options, and various toppings.

"This is overwhelming," Kiara said, looking over it. I agreed. Nearly the entire wall was covered in options.

"Yeah, it can be a lot," Elyssa admitted. "But to make it easier: you need to pick a cone or bowl, a base of ice cream, which can be one or two scoops, up to four toppings, and up to two sauces. It can be any combination that you want."

"That does not make it any easier," Kiara said, staring at the wall in awe.

There had been one person in line when we'd come in, but she'd moved off to the side to wait for her ice cream. I glanced over the menu quickly, surmised that there was no way that I would ever be able to make a decision, and went up to order.

"Hi there, how can I help you?" The worker asked.

"Hi, can have..." There was another menu behind her, so I just read off the first things I saw. "A waffle cone with mint chocolate chip ice cream please?"

"Of course!" She said. She spoke in a bright voice that reminded me of Bree. There was a pang in my heart for a reason that I didn't quite understand. "Any toppings?"

"Yes." I glanced over the list and once again read out the first things I saw. "Um, brownie bits, cherries, miniature marshmallows, and rainbow sprinkles, please."

"Great! And any sauces?"

"Fudge sauce, please." I glanced at the order total then handed over the money. "You can keep the change."

"Thank you very much! Please wait at the end of the counter."

I nodded and did so. Bree went up after me to order her ice cream then came to wait next to me. We didn't get a chance to talk before we each had an ice cream cone handed to us. We moved back over to where Harlee, Kiara, and Elyssa were still studying the menu.

"Have you decided what you want?" I asked them. They all shook their heads.

"There are too many choices!" Kiara said. Bree made a sympathetic noise.

Another group walked into the shop. Bree and I moved over to the left side of the shop so that we weren't blocking the view of the menu. With both our groups in there, the small shop felt a little crowded. A minute later, another group entered as well, and the shop became a little more crowded than I was comfortable with. I was actually a little concerned it might be a fire hazard. I ended up with my back pressed against the wall, desperately trying not to let my ice cream fall out of the cone.

"Maybe we should wait outside," Bree suggested. Somebody elbowed me as they walked past and I nearly dropped my ice cream.

"Yeah, I think that's a good idea," I said.

"We'll meet you out there once we've ordered," Elyssa said.

"Okay, no rush!" Bree said. We went outside and sat on a bench in front of the shop. Neither of us looked at each other. I stared at the ground, and from what I could tell, Bree was looking around as if the town was the most interesting place she had ever seen. This was the first time we'd been properly alone since getting out of the water the night before.

"What flavour ice cream did you get?" She asked eventually.

"I don't even remember," I said. "I really just pointed at random things on the menu."

She laughed. My heart warmed at the sound.

"Mine is a weird flavour," she said. "I can't even

remember the name anymore. I think it's a mix of a bunch of stuff."

"Like rocky road?" I asked.

"Yeah, something like that," she agreed.

I nodded, still looking at the ground. I would have said something to spare us the awkward silence if I had anything to say.

After a minute, she sighed. "We should talk about what happened last night."

"There's nothing to talk about," I said. "We just went skinny dipping, like plenty of friends do, and that's all."

"I..." Her breath hitched. I looked up. She was staring at me intently. "I had a lot of fun last night, April... I'm really glad we did all this."

We stared at each other for a moment. Everything felt perfect between us — and how could something that felt so right ever be wrong? We leaned towards each other. My eyes fluttered shut. We were moments away from kissing—

"Hey, guys!" Elyssa called. My eyes shot open again. She was walking towards us. "What are you doing?"

She was going to know. She was going to know that I liked Bree and that I was about to kiss her and everything would fall apart. I needed to turn her attention away from what Bree and I were doing.

So, in a moment of panic, my arm shot forward to push Bree away from me. Except that hand was the one holding my ice cream cone, so instead of pushing her away, I shoved my ice cream straight into her face.

"April!" Bree screamed. I pulled my hand back quickly, horrified at what I'd done. Unfortunately, my cone came back empty, as the whole scoop of ice cream was on her face.

"I am so sorry!" I exclaimed. I had a couple of napkins that I got with my ice cream, so I handed them to her to wipe the ice cream off her face. "I am so sorry, Bree! I did not mean to do that."

"What did you mean to do?" Elyssa laughed. Bree easily wiped most of the ice cream off her face, though there was still a little smeared against her light skin. To my relief, she was laughing as well.

"I don't know," I lied. "I guess my arm just twitched or something."

They both seemed to accept this excuse and laughed along. But when Bree and I made eye contact, I saw in her eyes that I hadn't imagined everything that just happened between us.

I couldn't believe what I'd done. I was mad at myself for letting my guard down for just long enough to almost kiss Bree. But even more than that, I was mad at Elyssa for stopping me.

❧ 24 ❧

WHEN WE WENT CLIFF JUMPING, Bree told me to just run and jump, but I kept chickening out when I got close to the edge. Luckily, I managed to stop myself early enough each time that I didn't somehow fall into the water, but I was pretty sure that I took another year off of Bree's life every time anyway.

"April, you're going to hurt yourself," she kept saying. "Stop overthinking it. Just run and jump."

It was easy enough for her to say. She'd learned to cliff jump years ago.

"I'm surprised you don't like this, April," Elyssa said. She was the only other one who came with us. "You normally love anything that gives you an adrenaline rush."

She was mostly right in that assessment, but also a little wrong. I loved adrenaline rushes, but I loved my safety and life more. Thus, I liked to do things that were enough to give me a rush without making me feel like my life was legitimately in danger — things like roller coasters, white water rafting, and zip-lining. Sometimes, even those were a little iffy due to the height component. Free falling off a cliff and hoping that I landed right and didn't hurt myself wasn't exactly my idea of a good time, no matter how much Elyssa and Bree insisted it was safe.

"It's just new," I said, even though that wasn't even close to the reason. "I don't know how to do it yet."

"You're psyching yourself out too much," Bree said. "You just need to run, jump, and take a deep breath before you hit the water. Trust me, you'll love it."

I did trust her, in more ways than one. I knew she wouldn't lead me astray. But actually going through with the jump was easier said than done.

"There's a reason I have this listed as conquer a fear," I said. "It's not exactly like I'm going to get over it in a second."

"Sorry," Bree said softly. "I didn't mean to diminish that."

I shook my head. "That wasn't what I meant. I just... need some time."

"Of course," Bree said. "Tale all the time you need."

I took a deep breath and stared at the cliff edge ahead. *It isn't that big of a deal,* I told myself. *Bree did it and she survived. Sure, the water will be cold. And sure, it will be kind of terrifying. But it will be okay.*

I looked at Bree. She smiled and gave me a thumbs up. Pure joy shone in my chest at her smile. Pure joy and, just for a moment, absolute fearlessness. And before I could talk myself out of it, I ran. I ran at full speed and before I could overthink it, I jumped. For those few glorious seconds that I flew through the air, I was weightless. Then I crashed through the cold and choppy waves below. My body sunk deep into the water. Bubbles surrounded me as I breathed out. My hair, which had been in a ponytail but now seemed to be flying loose, floated around me. I allowed myself to just sink for a few moments before I kicked my way back to the surface.

I swam to the shallow rocks at the edge of the lake. As I climbed out, Bree ran down the small path to meet me.

"How was it?" She asked. There was a huge smile on her face. The wind around us whipped her blonde hair against her face and made me shiver. I laughed loudly and pushed my hair back.

"Amazing," I said. "Absolutely amazing."

This was why I put *conquer a fear* down on that list. Because nothing felt as good as doing what you once thought was impossible.

25

WHEN WE WERE PACKING UP at the last motel, some of Bree's toiletries had somehow ended up in my bag. I'd been so tired the night before that I hadn't even noticed, and I guess she hadn't either. When we got back from cliff jumping, I went take a shower and noticed her stuff in there, so I grabbed it to take up to her.

Her bedroom door was wide open but the room looked empty. I knocked anyway and called, "Bree?"

"I'm in here!"

I walked further in and noticed that the bathroom door was open. Bree was standing inside, styling her now-dry hair.

"Hey," I said, walking inside. I held up the ziplock bag of stuff. "I found some of your stuff in my bag."

"Oh, thank you so much!" She said. She grabbed it from me and put it on the counter. "I was wondering where it got to."

I leaned against the door frame.

"Do you know when everyone else is supposed to get

back?" I asked. Bree and I had both wanted to come back to the cottage after cliff jumping, but Harlee and Kiara wanted to go into town, so Elyssa came back to drop us off and pick them up. They'd left about half an hour ago, but I wasn't sure how long they were planning on staying out. There wasn't all that much to do in town, honestly.

"Elyssa said they would only be gone an hour or two," Bree said.

"Okay." I glanced around her bathroom out of curiosity. For the most part, it was similar to mine with wood furnishing and dark fixtures, but it felt a little newer. I couldn't remember if this area of the cottage was part of the addition.

As I looked around, I noticed something green near the light on the wall above Bree's head from the corner of my eye. At first, I thought it was just the reflection of the light, but when I looked at it straight on, I realized it had wings. It was some kind of large green moth.

"What is that?" I asked.

"What?" Bree asked. I pointed at the bug. She looked over and immediately screamed so loud that I had to cover my ears. I was suddenly very glad that we were alone in the building.

"Get it out, get it out, get it out!" Bree cried. I wanted to help but I wasn't entirely sure how to get a giant moth out of a bathroom. Why was it in there in the first place in the middle of the day? Didn't moths only come out at night?

The only thing I knew about moths was that they were attracted to light, so I dove for the light switch. Although the sun was out, the blinds were shut so when

I turned off the lights, the bathroom was thrown into darkness. Luckily, the bedroom light was still on so the moth flew in that direction instead, and I slammed the bathroom door behind it. Then I turned the light back on.

Bree was standing with her back against the sink. Her hands were covering her mouth and her eyes were wide.

"I think I got rid of it," I said. Bree nodded silently.

"Thanks for that," she said in a small voice.

"Happy to help," I said. My breathing was oddly ragged as if getting rid of the moth was the most exercise I had done in weeks. Which, I supposed, it very well might have been.

"So, how are we going to leave now?" Bree asked slowly.

"Hm?"

"I mean, the moth is now in the bedroom. And that's the only exit."

"Right," I said. I thought it over for a moment, but the only other solution I could come up with was climbing out the window, which wasn't ideal seeing as we were on the second story of the house. "I have no idea. You?"

She shook her head. "Me neither."

"I guess we just have to make a run for it," I said. "We can open the window and close the bedroom door, and hope that it flies out."

Bree nodded. "Yeah. Yeah, that works."

She still looked a little worried, though. I had always thought being scared of bugs was a little stupid, but I felt bad that Bree was so freaked out and I wanted to fix it. I chose to ignore the implications of that.

"If you want, I can go first," I offered. "I can see if I can get rid of it."

"No, that's all right," she said, but I could tell that was what she wanted me to do.

"I don't mind," I said. I turned back around and tried to open the door. The keyword here being tried because the door handle wouldn't turn.

"What's the matter?" Bree asked.

"The door handle is stuck," I said. I pressed down with all my weight but it wouldn't move at all.

"Maybe try pulling it?" Bree suggested. "Some door handles aren't supposed to move."

I tried pulling but the door didn't move at all. In desperation, I then tried pushing at it, even though I knew it swung inwards.

"No, no, no!" I yelled. I slammed my hand against the door, then tried everything I had done again on the off chance that it would fix it, but of course, it didn't move. I sighed and rested my forehead against the cold wood. In a resigned voice, I said, "We're stuck."

"Well, it could be worse," Bree said with her usual optimism. I glanced back at her.

"How, Bree?" I asked. "How could it be worse? We're stuck in a bathroom with no phones or way of contacting anyone outside, while all our friends are out, and probably won't be back for at least another hour."

"We could be stuck in the bathroom of a dingy motel instead of this rather nice cottage."

Despite my annoyance at the whole situation, I laughed.

"I guess that's fair," I said. I walked to the other side of the room where Bree was standing and sat in front of the sink, with my back resting against the cupboard. Bree sat down next to me.

"So, what should we do in the meantime?" She asked.

I shrugged. "I think having an activity for literally every situation we could ever end up in is more your area of expertise."

"Right." Bree bit her lip and thought for a moment. "We could play I spy?"

"I cannot think of anything I would hate more than playing I spy right now."

"Okay smartass, what do you want to do?"

"I can think of one thing," I muttered. As soon as the words left my mouth, I wanted to take them back. I hadn't really meant to say it out loud. Things were already a little weird between us since the almost kiss situation — even if we were both trying to ignore it — and I certainly didn't want to make them any weirder.

Bree didn't respond. I was sure that I had freaked her out, which is the opposite of what you want to do when you are locked in a room with someone. Trying not to show the embarrassment on my face, I looked up.

Except Bree didn't look freaked out or angry. Only surprised.

Before I could understand what was happening, Bree leaned towards me. At first, I thought I was imagining it. Then, once my brain caught up to the fact that this was very much real, I was certain that I must be misinterpreting her actions. Then our lips collided, and I knew it was neither.

It was like everything I'd been dreaming of. Everything and more.

Bree's hand slid down my side until it landed on my

hip. I slowly fell back until I was lying on the floor with Bree on top of me. Okay, maybe not the most comfortable position, but I would take what I could get. She began kissing my neck as I wrapped my arm around her.

"This can't be real," I murmured. She pulled back a little. Her face hovered right over mine, her hair falling like a curtain around us.

"It is," she whispered. Then she kissed me again.

Her lips were soft against my skin as she worked her way down my body. Cold air blew on me as she pulled off my skirt. I threaded my fingers through her hair as she did to me what I could only describe as magic.

Then, out of the blue, she froze. I groaned, itching to feel her again.

"What are you doing?" I asked. I twisted my head so I could see her. Her eyes flitted around the room.

"Did you hear that?" She whispered. I listened for a moment, but all I heard was our breathing.

"Hear what?" I asked.

As if on cue, the door handle jiggled. The door didn't open, just as it hadn't when I tried to open it from this side, though I was happy about it this time. My heart pounded in my chest. Somebody knocked on the other side.

"Bree?" Kiara called. "Are you in there?"

Bree and I locked eyes. My stomach dropped. I hadn't even heard the others get home.

"What do I say?" Bree whispered.

"I don't know!" I whispered back. She sat up properly. I felt empty without her there but I didn't say anything.

"I have to say something or she'll get suspicious," she

hissed. I shrugged helplessly. At a normal volume, she said, "Uh, yeah, I'm in here. What do you need?"

"I was just looking for my hairbrush," she replied. "Do you mind if I come in?"

Bree looked to me, her eyes wide with panic. My pulse was racing, this time for different reasons. All I could imagine is Kiara walking into the bathroom expecting to see Bree brushing her teeth or something, and instead find me lying there half-naked, with her between legs.

"The door is stuck!" Bree exclaimed in a strangled voice. I sighed in relief. I was so caught up in the moment that I'd completely forgotten why we were in this position in the first place.

"Oh," Kiara said. She jiggled the door handle again. "That's weird. I'll see if Elyssa knows how to fix it."

"Great, thanks!" Bree said. Her voice cracked halfway through it.

I waited until the receding footsteps disappeared before I dared to breathe again.

"What the hell are we going to do now?" I asked. I sat up as well and pulled my skirt back on, then leaned against the bathtub. "If they get that door open and find us stuck in the bathroom together, they're going to have a lot of questions!"

"I know!" Bree said. She grabbed her hair in her fists. "I guess we can just tell them the truth? There is a completely reasonable explanation for the whole thing."

"It would probably be easier to explain if we weren't both completely flushed red," I pointed out. "And if I had said something when Kiara asked if you were in here."

"Right," Bree said. Her face fell. "Unfortunately, coming up with lies is not my strong suit."

"It's not exactly mine either," I muttered. That wasn't entirely true — I was pretty good at coming up with simple lies, but something as elaborate as a reasonable explanation as to why I was locked in a bathroom with Bree, looking like I had just hooked up with someone, and didn't say anything when Kiara came by was a bit above my pay grade.

"We could tell them you didn't want to make it weird by saying you were in here," Bree suggested. "And that we look flushed because... I don't know. Maybe they'll take so long to open the door that it won't even be noticeable by then."

"Maybe," I agreed, mainly to make her feel better.

We both fell silent, as we considered how on earth to get out of this predicament. My only idea was once again to climb out the window, but that did not feel like a very good plan.

Suddenly, Bree snapped and pointed her fingers at me.

"I know!" She said excitedly. "We'll tell them you fell asleep."

I blinked a couple of times. I was sure that I'd heard her wrong — after all, how was that going to fix any of this?

"Oh?" I asked neutrally. I didn't want to stomp all over her idea, especially if there was more to it than she had told me, but I also didn't know how to act positively towards a plan that thus far made no sense to me.

"Yeah," she said. She nodded really fast and enthusi-astically. A couple of locks of hair fell in her face, and without thinking, I tucked them back behind her ear. She faltered a little, the touch distracting her. "Um, I mean, we'll go with the original story of how we ended up in here. Then we'll just say it got really warm and we weren't sure how long they were going to be gone, so you took a nap. And maybe I did too. That's why I was acting so weird when Kiara came by, and why you didn't say anything."

It wasn't the best lie I'd ever heard but it was better than anything I could come up with so I agreed.

There was another knock on the door.

"Hey, Bree." It was Elyssa's voice. "Sorry I forgot to warn you that this door gets stuck sometimes. Give me a minute, I'll get it open."

"Okay, thanks," Bree said. She looked at me nervously. "Just so you know, April's in here too."

"April?" I could just imagine the confused look on her face. "Why?"

"She was helping me get rid of a bug and slammed the door shut," Bree explained. "That's when the door got stuck."

There was some muffled laughter from the other side of the door.

"Oh," Elyssa said. The latch clicked, and the door swung open. Elyssa walked inside. "There you go. It usually doesn't get stuck like that unless you slam it, which is why I didn't think to mention it to you."

Oh. My bad.

"Thanks so much, Elyssa," Bree said. She jumped to her feet.

"Why didn't you call one of us to help you?" Elyssa asked. Her eyes roamed over each of us like she was looking for a sign of something. I didn't like it. Even though I was sure she didn't know what had just taken place in that room, I felt like she knew all my secrets.

"Neither of us had our phones," Bree said. "And we couldn't yell because you were out, so we just hung out in here."

"Took a nap," I supplied. Elyssa looked like she was fighting back laughter as she nodded along.

"Fair," she said. She gestured to the open doorway. "We brought food back with us if you're hungry."

"Oh, I'm starving," Bree said. I was also pretty hungry but I didn't really want to go sit with my friends and pretend everything was normal quite yet.

"I never got the chance to take a shower," I said. "I'd like to do that first."

"Okay," Elyssa said. "Do you mind if we go ahead and eat without you? I can leave your food in the fridge."

"Yeah, that's completely fine," I said. It was probably ideal, actually, since it meant I wouldn't have to sit down for a meal with them until breakfast at the earliest.

I walked to my room down the hall while Bree and Elyssa went downstairs, speaking amicably. I was amazed at Bree's ability to act as if everything was normal when it so clearly wasn't.

I went into my own ensuite bathroom and closed the door behind me. I stared at myself in the mirror and wondered what the hell I had just done.

The guest room in Elyssa's house was significantly more comfortable than any motel we'd stayed in, but I couldn't fall asleep that night. As I laid in the dark, all I could think about was everything that happened between me and Bree that afternoon.

In the moment, it had all felt so right. But it could never happen again.

While dating somebody who used to be just a friend sounded good on paper, I knew it would only lead to heartbreak. It would ruin my friendship with Bree, and would ruin the dynamic of our friend group as a whole. We had too many close calls already, with Elyssa almost seeing us kiss, and her and Kiara nearly finding out about what happened in the bathroom.

I couldn't be with Bree — I knew that. So why couldn't I stop thinking about her?

❧ 26 ❧

I BARELY SLEPT THAT NIGHT. Instead, I stayed up worrying about how on earth I was going to navigate talking to Bree about everything that happened between us. There was obviously a lot for us to unpack and I wasn't sure how we could manage it without somebody's feelings getting hurt.

I tried to push the thoughts away in the morning as I got ready for the day. But once I was dressed and ready to go, I ended up lying back down on my made bed. I glanced at the clock. It was already mid-morning. Normally, I would be up and getting breakfast by this point, but I had no desire to leave my room. Leaving my room meant having to be near Bree and that was not something I wanted to do yet. I didn't particularly want to be near any of my other friends either for that matter. I wasn't sure I could look them in the eyes yet after everything that happened the day before.

I knew I should at least go find Bree, though. We needed to talk about what had happened and putting it off wasn't going to help anyone. I was just preparing myself to do so when there was a light knock on my door. When I looked over, I saw Bree standing in my doorway, shifting her weight from foot to foot.

She was dressed pretty casually and her hair was wet like she had just gotten out of the shower. I wondered if she had also been avoiding going downstairs.

"Hey," she said. "Can I come in?"

"Of course," I said. I wasn't looking forward to the conversation but I knew we needed to have it at some point, and it was probably better sooner rather than later.

I pushed myself up and moved so I was sitting near the head of the bed, and she sat at the foot. It didn't escape my notice that she sat on the very edge of the bed with her feet planted on the ground like she was ready to make a run for it at any moment.

"So," Bree said. She sighed and clasped her hands together. "We need to talk about yesterday."

"Yes," I said. She didn't continue speaking, so I decided I might as well start the conversation. "I've been thinking about it a lot since it happened..."

"Yeah?" Bree said. She was frowning. I think she was worried about where I was going with it. I was worried about how she was going to react to what I was going to say.

"I wanted to make it clear that I didn't really think what we did was a big deal," I said. "It was just sex. And it only happened because of the circumstances."

Bree nodded so fast that I felt like her head was going to snap off.

"Exactly," she said.

Of course, I found Bree attractive. I think that much was very obvious to both of us. But it wasn't anything deeper than that and it never had been. I must have tricked myself into thinking I was interested in her romantically because I found her attractive and wanted to be with her.

"I don't have feelings for you," I said. "Not in that way. You're my friend."

"I agree," Bree said. She looked relieved. "It was just a one-time thing, and we never need to talk about it again."

I nodded. I was glad to see that she agreed with me. I thought about what Harlee had said at the gas station about me and Bree making a good couple and my argument against it.

"We would never work as a couple anyway," I said. "We're way too different."

"Oh absolutely," Bree said. She smiled at me. "We both know I'm way too high maintenance for you."

I laughed and nodded.

This was good. Now that we'd had this discussion, we could go back to normal.

So why did everything still feel so wrong?

❧ 27 ❧

WE WENT CAMPING the next day. We decided to stay at Elyssa's cottage for a few days then drive straight to Algonquin in one day, rather than stopping at motels in between since her place was nicer (and obviously cheaper) than anywhere else we could stay.

It wasn't a particularly long drive to Algonquin, but it was through the countryside, with only Elyssa's shitty directions to guide us once again. My first plan was for Elyssa to drive part of it since she had her driver's license too, but she quickly informed me that there was no way she could drive my car. Still, I thought having her in the car would make the process easier since she could just tell me where to go, but it turns out, it was even worse. She tried directing us as we went along but it would be something like, "I think this is the turn. Oh wait, maybe it's the next one. Yes, it's definitely the next one. No, never mind it was that one and we missed it." Needless to say, it was extremely stressful, and by the time Bree and I decided to switch drivers, I was ready to scream.

"Sorry," Bree said. "I should have just driven the whole thing."

I shook my head. "You were tired. I didn't mind driving this part."

I was lying through my teeth and we both knew it, but she nodded.

It was around then that I decided I was just going to pretend nothing had happened between us. I had only been physically attracted to her and I acted on that now, so there was no reason for me to still act like someone with a crush whenever I was around her. And as for the act itself, I was sure that plenty of people have sex with their friends then go back to normal and pretend it didn't happen, so I was just doing the same. Nothing had to be weird.

We got to the campsite in the early evening. The first thing we did was set up our tents before we all got too tired to do it. I was sharing a tent with Bree and Elyssa, while Kiara and Harlee shared the other tent. I unfortunately kept getting paired up with Bree for everything since I couldn't find a good way to argue it.

Once it was finally late enough, we started a campfire to cook dinner over. Bree and I sat together on one log, with Kiara and Harlee on the log to our right, and Elyssa to our left.

"Okay, I was skeptical about cooking burgers over a campfire," Harlee said, as we finished eating, "but this is actually really good."

"I told you," Kiara said. Kiara always sang the praises of camping.

"I want dessert," Bree said, bouncing her legs up and down.

"I'll grab the brownie mix from the car!" Kiara said. She came back a second later with the brownie mix box, a large metal pot, and a spatula in hand.

"So small issue," she said. She put both items down as she sat. "Well, two actually. First, we only have this giant pot to make it in. Second, we totally forgot that brownie mix needs eggs and didn't bring any. So these brownies definitely won't cook."

"So, let's not cook them," Elyssa said with a shrug.

"What do you mean?" Kiara asked.

"Let's just eat the batter," Elyssa explained.

"It's not safe to eat batter," Harlee said.

"Yeah, because of the eggs," Elyssa said. "It should be fine without it."

"The flour is also dangerous," Harlee said.

"It will probably be fine," Kiara said dismissively. "Let's do it!"

Harlee shrugged. "All right. Don't blame me if you get sick."

Kiara tore open the box and dumped the powder into the pot. Elyssa handed her a full water bottle.

"How much water am I supposed to use?" Kiara asked.

"Just eyeball it," Elyssa said.

"Okay," Kiara said. She took the lid off the bottle and poured a good amount of water into the pot as well. Then, she grabbed a spatula and mixed it. I cringed as I watched it. "Alright, I think that's good."

"Where are the spoons?" Elyssa asked, looking around.

"Oh, I forgot to grab them from the car," Kiara said. "I'll get them now."

"Wait," Bree said. "I have a better idea."

I was worried by the look in her eyes.

"What is it?" I asked.

"We pour the batter instead of eating with the spoon."

"What, like drink it?" Kiara asked. "The pot is probably too big for us to hold like that."

"Not if somebody else pours it for us. Like, I'll sit or kneel or whatever and April pours it for me."

There were so many jokes I could make about that but I didn't want to make Bree uncomfortable.

"Let's do it!" Kiara said. Harlee looked less enthused about the idea but I know she'd go along with it because Kiara was doing it.

"Okay!" Elyssa said.

Bree, Elyssa, and Kiara all stood up. Bree grabbed my hands and pulled me to my feet.

"Come on, come on, let's go!" She said. Harlee stood up as well and grabbed the metal pot.

"We should do it on the rocks so we don't get chocolate everywhere," Harlee said.

We went over to the large rocks by the water. Bree went on her knees, and Harlee handed me the metal pot.

"Ready?" I asked. Bree nodded. I tipped it until the batter began pouring out into Bree's mouth. It all went well for the first ten seconds or so, but then Bree stared to move. She moved around so much that instead of the batter going into her mouth, it spilled all over her face, her hair, and her clothes. She finally moved far enough away that the batter wasn't getting on her anymore. I'm sad to admit that it didn't occur to me until she was completely covered in chocolate that I probably should have put the pot down the second she started moving.

Luckily, Bree came up laughing, and the rest of us soon joined in.

"What the hell were you doing?" I asked Bree.

"My mouth was full!" She said. She tried to wipe the chocolate off her face but it smeared all over. I was reminded of when I shoved my ice cream into her face and I cringed at the memory.

"So why didn't you just make some kind of hand motion to tell me to stop?"

"I didn't think you would understand! I thought you would stop when you noticed that you were pouring chocolate all over me."

"Evidently she didn't," Harlee said dryly. "Maybe we should come up with a hand motion to do before the next person goes so this doesn't happen again."

Harlee had a way of speaking that made you feel like you were a complete idiot. Oftentimes, it annoyed me, but this time, I had to admit that she had a point.

"Who wants to go next?" Elyssa asked.

"I will," Harlee said. She and Bree switched spots.

"My arms are tired from holding it," I said. "Does somebody else want to do it?'

"You only held it for like a minute!" Kiara said.

"It was heavy!" I defended. In all honesty, I was probably the worst person to be in charge of it because I was extremely physically unfit.

"I can do it," Elyssa offered. I tried to ignore the way that she picked up the pot with ease. "Ready, Harlee?"

"Wait," Harlee said. She thought for a moment. "Okay, I'll wave my hand when I want you to stop, okay?"

Elyssa nodded. And to Harlee's credit, she didn't end up covered in chocolate like Bree, so her plan was definitely the better one.

"Do either of you want a go?" Elyssa asked, looking at me and Kiara.

Kiara nodded and went next. She did the same motion as Harlee did to indicate when to stop and it worked well. I went up next.

"I'm probably going to end up blanking on what hand motion to do," I said as I kneeled. The rock was uncomfortable and a little painful under my legs, making just want to get this over with.

Elyssa grinned. "At least Bree will be in good company, then."

"Here, I can pour it," Bree said. She looked at me. "And unlike you, I will actually stop pouring it if you move at all."

I narrowed my eyes. I didn't like the look on her face. I hoped that Elyssa would say that it was okay and she could do it herself, but she just gave Bree the container without any argument.

And, of course, Bree missed my mouth and poured chocolate all over my head. Or perhaps missed is the wrong word. It was more like she tipped the container upside down and purposefully doused me in brownie mix.

"Bree!" I yelled, as all my friends cracked up laughing. My vision was blocked by chocolate. The more I tried to brush the chocolate away, the more it got in my eyes, and I was thankful that years of swimming without goggles made my eyes less sensitive. Luckily, after a few seconds, it began to drip away, allowing me to see a little. I ran my hands through my hair, which was completely doused in chocolate. I guess it was good revenge for me pouring batter on her and smashing my ice cream against her face.

"Oops," Bree said, a grin playing on her lips.

Oops.

A piece of me wanted to get angry, to scream at her for getting chocolate all over me. But I pushed that part of me down. I knew she didn't do it to be vindictive, and honestly, I probably did deserve it.

More than anything, I was happy to see her laughing.

❧ 28 ❧

I WASN'T SURE what time I fell asleep, but it did not feel like I'd slept for nearly long enough when I woke up.

"April, wake up."

I finally opened my eyes just a crack. Bree was kneeling next to me with her hands on my shoulders. For one brief moment, I felt like we were alone at the cottage again, but it went away after a moment as I woke up properly.

"What do you want, Bree?" I groaned. I rubbed a hand over my face.

"The sun hasn't risen yet," she whispered.

"Great. Thanks for letting me know." I rolled over so I was facing away from her and closed my eyes again to go back to sleep, but she yanked me back. I kept my eyes tightly shut in protest.

"Don't you want to watch the sunrise?" Bree asked.

"Not if it means getting up right now," I muttered. She shook my shoulders again.

"April, watching the sunrise is the second last thing

on your list," she whispered forcefully. That finally got through to me. I still didn't particularly want to get up but it was just enough to get me to open my eyes and sit up.

I yawned. "Fine. Let me get something a little warmer on."

Bree smiled. "I'll wait outside."

She climbed back over Elyssa, who was somehow still sleeping soundly, and went outside the tent. I was tempted to go back to sleep now that she wasn't there to wake me up, but I knew that she would come back in and wake me up like some sort of human snooze button. So with a resigned sigh, I changed into a sweatshirt, sweatpants, and thick wool socks, and climbed outside as well.

Bree was waiting right outside the tent, with a large blanket wrapped around her shoulders. Although I was wearing some pretty warm clothes, the cold air bit into me.

"I was thinking we could sit on the rocks by the lake," Bree said. I nodded, still too tired to speak. We walked over and sat down. The rock was cold but then, so was everything else. Bree sat right next to me then shifted the blanket around so it covered both of us instead of just her. The butterflies in my stomach returned, but I told myself I was just hungry or something because I didn't like Bree like that.

"Thanks," I said softly.

"Don't mention it."

I think Bree was tired too because she didn't speak much either as we sat there and watched the sunrise over the lake. After the first couple of minutes, she rested her head on my shoulder and leaned some of her weight into me. I didn't say anything but my heart warmed at the action.

I wondered if maybe everything would be okay between us after all.

☙❧

"I can't believe nobody else is awake still," Bree said, about an hour after we'd gotten up. I considered saying that I wouldn't be up either if she hadn't dragged me out since this was the limited time I had without Jean waking me up at dawn, but I worried that might make her feel bad.

"None of us are really morning people," I said.

"Yeah, you can say that again," Bree said. She looked around the campsite. Her eyes landed on the overturned canoe sitting by the shore. Elyssa had insisted that we should bring it with us from her cottage. We'd attached it to the top of my car for the drive then brought it down to sit in its current place the first night we'd gotten there, but we hadn't used it yet. "Do you know how to canoe?"

"I've gone a few times," I said. "Why?"

"It just seems like an awful waste to have the canoe sitting there without any of us using it."

"Do you know how to canoe?"

"Kind of? I mean, I can paddle. But I don't know how to steer."

I wasn't particularly good at that part of canoeing either, but I figured I could do it well enough if we stayed close to shore.

"I can do it," I said.

Bree's face brightened. "Really?"

I nodded. "I mean, it's been a couple of years since I've gone canoeing, but I imagine it's like riding a bike, right?"

"Yeah, probably." She jumped to her feet and started walking to the canoe. I followed after her. "Do we have life jackets?"

"Um..." I looked around the campsite, but even if we did have them, nothing was out anyway. There was a possibility we had a couple somewhere, I figured Elyssa probably would have thought to pack them, but I didn't know where to begin looking. "It's fine, we don't need them. We'll stay close."

Bree looked a little worried about that plan but she shrugged it off. We flipped the canoe over so it was upright and slid it a little into the water. Luckily, it was facing the right direction so I wouldn't have to turn us around after we pushed off.

"You can climb in. I can push it out into the water with you in it," I said. Normally, I would have just said we could wade into the water and climb in there but neither of us were dressed for that. Bree nodded and sat down in the bow seat. I pushed the canoe out most of the way, then climbed in myself. I pushed us off from the shore using my paddle.

"Where do you want to go?" Bree asked.

I shrugged, then realized she couldn't see me.

"Doesn't matter to me," I said. "We can just go along the shoreline if you want. Or just in a circle around here."

It was probably best that we didn't go far given that

we weren't wearing life jackets and our friends didn't even know that we were in the canoe, let alone where we were going.

"Let's just hang around here," Bree said. We both paddled with relaxed, easy strokes. It was really nice to be out in the boat that early in the morning. The water was calm and the world was silent.

We were about twenty feet out of the shore when Bree stopped paddling.

"What's up?" I asked.

"Let's just sit for a few minutes," she said. I couldn't see her face since I was behind her, but I imagined that she had a very introspective look on her face.

"Okay," I said.

"Do you think I could turn around without tipping the canoe?"

"Uh, probably?" I honestly had no idea. "Just be careful."

She nodded. Very slowly, she turned to the side. Then she moved her right leg over and then her left leg. The boat rocked slightly but it didn't tip. Finally, she managed to turn all the way around until she was facing me. She grinned triumphantly. I couldn't help but smile back.

"Can I ask you a question?" She asked.

I resisted the urge to use the classic dad response of *you just did*.

"Of course."

"Was this trip everything you dreamed it would be?"

I had assumed she was going to ask something about canoeing, so the question took me by surprise. I thought about it. I knew she was asking about the road trip as a whole, but every memory that passed through my mind at that moment was of me and her. Everything unexpected that we'd been through on this road trip together. I hadn't dreamed about that, I hadn't the time to dream about it, but if I had, would this be everything I'd thought it would be? Was it worth it even when I knew that nothing more could come of it?

"Even better," I whispered.

29

SINCE I'D BEEN WOKEN up by Bree so early that morning, I was pretty tired all day. I tried to take a nap in the middle of the day, but it wasn't very feasible to do so when the tent didn't block out any sunlight. So, I would have thought that I would be out like a light by the time that I tried to fall asleep that night but unfortunately, that wasn't the case.

I'd been tossing and turning in my sleeping bag for probably close to twenty minutes when Bree murmured, "Can't sleep?"

I stilled. "Sorry, I didn't mean to wake you up."

"You didn't." She turned her head so she was facing me. "I can't sleep either."

"Me neither," Elyssa said from the other side of Bree. I almost jumped in shock. How did I not realize that both my tent mates were awake? "Maybe there's something in the air."

Obviously, it wasn't ideal that none of us could sleep,

but I did feel comforted by the fact that I wasn't the only one.

"What should we do to pass the time?" Bree asked.

"What can we do?" I asked. "It's not like we can watch TV or anything."

"We could go stargazing," Elyssa suggested.

"It's going to be so cold out," Bree sighed.

"But it will be pretty," I said. I opted not to point out that it was probably no colder than it had been that morning when we had shared her blanket. I doubted either of us wanted to do that with Elyssa there too. "I bet you can really see the stars out here."

Bree sighed deeply. For a moment, I thought she was going to say no. But then she sat up and said, "Yeah, okay, let's go."

We all climbed out of the tent. Luckily, I was still dressed in my warm clothes so I didn't freeze as soon as I walked outside. The night was silent save for the small waves crashing against the shore and the occasional rustling sound from the forest. It felt wrong to be making any noise in the calm atmosphere so I remained quiet as we walked. We went to the rocks since there were no trees there, giving us an unobstructed view of the sky.

We were just getting comfortable when I heard the sound of a zipper opening. For one panicked moment, I thought someone — or something — was getting into our tent, but then I realized the sound was coming from Kiara and Harlee's tent.

"Hey guys," Harlee said quietly. She laid down next to me, and Kiara next to her. "What are you doing?"

"None of us could sleep so we decided to do some

stargazing," Elyssa explained. "What are you two doing up?"

Harlee shrugged. Her shoulder brushed against mine.

"Same," she said.

We fell into silence again. The night sky was clear, giving us a beautiful view of the stars. I tried to identify some constellations but I had always been hopeless at doing so.

Something soft brushed against my hand. I glanced down, unsure of what it was. Bree laced her fingers between mine. My heart warmed.

I turned my head properly to look at her. I thought she would turn to look at me too, my breath must have been tickling her neck, but she was staring steadfastly at the stars. My eyes drifted back down to our intertwined hands, nestled neatly between our bodies, and I smiled to myself.

Shit. I'm falling in love with this girl.

30

WE LEFT ALGONQUIN the next morning. There seemed to be some unspoken agreement between Bree and me that we would not discuss anything that happened between us the past few days, including holding hands while staring at the night sky.

After all, in what world was that not romantic?

We were all pretty tired, so we didn't do anything but drive straight to a motel for the night. Once we'd paid for our rooms and put all our stuff inside, we all piled into the room I was sharing with Elyssa (thankfully, Harlee and Kiara suggested that they could have the three-person room that night since they'd had the two-person tent for the past two nights, so Bree was staying with them).

"What should we do for dinner?" Harlee asked. We had a map of the abysmally small town laid out flat in front of us.

"I can go pick up some take-out from town," Bree offered.

"I can go with you," Kiara said.

"Me too," Elyssa said.

"I'm not sure we need three people to pick up food," Bree laughed.

"I'm just bored," Kiara said.

"Same," Elyssa said.

Bree shrugged. "Okay, sure."

"What food are you going to get?" Harlee asked.

"Pizza?" Kiara suggested. She pointed to the Domino's listed on the map. We all nodded.

"All right, let's head out," Bree said. "Same order as usual?"

"Yeah, that works," Harlee said.

"All right," Bree said. "We'll see you later."

I tossed Bree the keys, and the three of them walked outside. The room went quiet. Harlee moved from where she'd been sitting on the bed to lay on her stomach on the floor. I was a little confused as to why she was doing that until I looked over properly and realized she was reading. She frequently read in very strange positions that she claimed were comfortable, so this was actually pretty tame. She had the paperback cover folded back, so I had to shift a little to see the title. Of course, it was *To Kill a Mockingbird*. It was her favourite book; the spine was cracked and the cover was nearly falling off because of how many times she'd read it.

I pulled out my phone and scrolled through social media to pass the time, not wanting to disturb her. About ten minutes passed before she even shifted slightly.

"What's going on with you and Bree?" Harlee asked

out of the blue. I looked up from my phone, my heart pounding.

"What?" I asked as innocently as possible. It couldn't be that obvious, could it? "What do you mean? Nothing is going on between us."

She rolled her eyes. "Cut the crap, April. I can see the way you two have been acting."

"How have we been acting?" My voice was strained even to my own ears.

She stared at me, obviously unimpressed.

"You're obviously interested in each other," she said. I gulped. "So why haven't you done anything?"

I tried to laugh it off like I had at the gas station. But things had changed so much between then and now that I couldn't feasibly convince her that I thought the very idea of me and Bree being together was ludicrous anymore.

"Again," I said, "nothing is going on between me and Bree. We're just friends. We would never work as a couple."

Harlee rolled her eyes. "Quit lying to me, April."

I glanced at the clock surreptitiously. Kiara, Elyssa, and Bree had only gone out recently and wouldn't be back soon enough for me to get away with evading her questions like this. And realistically, even if they did somehow come back soon and save me, Harlee would follow up on it later — when she wanted something, she got it.

"You can't tell anyone," I said seriously. The last thing I needed was Kiara and Elyssa getting on our case about this.

Harlee raised an eyebrow but she nodded.

"I'm very good at keeping secrets," she said. I believed her wholeheartedly.

"Bree and I hooked up at Elyssa's cottage," I said. Apparently, that wasn't what Harlee was expecting. Her jaw dropped ever-so-slightly, which for her was like screaming.

"You what?" She asked.

"I thought you knew we did something!" I said. "That's what you made it sound like."

"I could tell that something happened between the two of you but I didn't expect that!"

I sighed and pushed my hair back with my fingers. I was already regretting this conversation.

"It wasn't a big deal," I said. "It was just... we were locked in the bathroom together and—"

"Wait, that's what you were doing in the bathroom?" Harlee asked in disbelief.

I blushed. "Uh, yeah. But it wasn't on purpose! I mean, we didn't go in there with the intention— we accidentally got locked in the bathroom, and one thing led to another."

"And you hooked up with her," Harlee said in a flat voice.

"Forget it," I muttered. I picked at my fingernails. I shouldn't have told her; I should have just said that Bree and I had an argument or something, and that's why we were acting so weird, even if that was the opposite of what really happened. "I wouldn't expect you to understand."

Harlee sighed. "No, I'm sorry. That wasn't the best way for me to react. Explain it to me."

"Explain what, Harlee?" I asked. I spread my hands.

"I hooked up with Bree and now everything's weird between us. That's all."

"No." She shook her head. "No, that's not all. This started way before we got to Elyssa's cottage. You've been acting weird the whole road trip."

"What, you mean when you joked about Bree and I being a couple?" I asked. "That wasn't anything."

"I only asked about that because of how you were acting around her! And besides, you practically admitted to me that you had a crush on her after we found the two of you cuddling."

I wanted to argue but I wasn't sure what I could say to that. She wasn't wrong.

"Yeah, I had a crush on her," I muttered. I snapped my mouth shut again. I hadn't meant to let that out.

"You did?" Harlee asked. I didn't understand why she was surprised. I wondered if Harlee just liked to act like she knew everything already to get people to tell her things.

"Yeah," I said. I'd already admitted the turn so I figured I might as well keep going. "I, uh, I started to catch feelings just before we left on the road trip. And I tried to convince myself that it wasn't true, that they weren't there, but it kept growing stronger. And then we got locked in the bathroom and... everything just felt so right, you know?"

"But then it went wrong again," she murmured.

"We agreed that it should just be a one-time thing. Which is absolutely for the best! But when we were in Algonquin, it all felt different."

"It can be hard to go back to being friends after being something more," Harlee said.

"Yeah, that's what I'm afraid of," I muttered. "If I confess my feelings, then it will ruin the friendship."

Harlee tilted her head. "Why do you say that?"

I bit my lip and thought about what to tell her. I had never really told anyone the extent of what happened between me and my ex-girlfriend. I preferred to leave the past in the past. But there was no way for me to explain my feelings now without telling her the whole story — if I didn't explain my reasoning, then she would probably just think I was stupid for not wanting to tell Bree, and that wouldn't help the situation at all. Besides, I thought it might be nice to finally tell somebody the story. And Harlee did say she was good at keeping secrets.

"When I started middle school, I made this really good friend named Tina," I said. Saying her name hurt me a little, even when I hadn't spoken to her in a couple of years. Harlee nodded, clearly not understanding what this had to do with our previous conversation. "Then, in grade ten, we started dating. It was pretty low-key at first, but obviously, it got more serious with time. She was with me for everything and I, being a naive fifteen-year-old, thought that we were probably going to get married one day. It all seemed good until it wasn't anymore. In early grade twelve, we broke up. The break-up in and of itself was devastating, but then on top of that it ruined our friendship."

"And you never fixed it?" Harlee asked quietly.

"No," I said. "I haven't spoken to her since that day. Not really. It also tore apart our entire friend group. It wasn't even a situation where they all chose one of us — everyone got wrapped up into the break-up too much, so suddenly, it was like I was breaking up with all of them instead of just her."

"And you're scared that's what is going to happen to us," Harlee said. She rested her chin against her fist. "That if you and Bree started dating and then you break up, it might tear apart our whole friend group."

"Exactly," I said. "And it wasn't just what happened with Tina, either. Once I finally got over her and actually made some new friends, I started to get feelings for another friend. It took me a while to get the courage to ask her out but then once I did... she didn't want anything to do with me anymore."

"Was she straight?" Harlee asked. The question took me by surprise, though I suppose it shouldn't have. How many times had I heard from other gay girls that their straight friends were terrified of them catching feelings for them?

"No," I said. "No, she was very much into girls. She just wasn't into me."

Harlee stayed quiet for a minute. Then another. I started to get uncomfortable with the silence, like I should say something but I didn't have anything to say.

"Bree's into you," she said, after a few minutes. "I know she is."

I shook my head. "You can't know that."

"I can see it, April," Harlee insisted.

"And I thought I saw it in my friend!" I snapped. I took a deep breath. "Look, sometimes we see what we want to see. And there's no way you can tell me with one hundred per cent certainty that Bree is interested in me."

"You two literally hooked up a few days ago."

"And we both agreed it was a one-time thing that we

will never do again," I retorted. "She probably just thinks it was a mistake."

"Do you?" She asked.

I looked away.

Harlee sighed. "April... Bree isn't like your old friend. She's not going to stop talking to you just because you admit your feelings. It doesn't have to end that way."

I shook my head. "It always does."

There was nothing she could do that would ever convince me otherwise.

31

THE GOOD PART about switching up room assignments every night was that it meant that there were some nights that I didn't share a room with Bree at all, which was definitely the best for my own sanity. On the flip side, though, it meant that there were some nights that I ended up sharing a room alone with Bree, which happened the night after I talked to Harlee.

I would have assumed that Harlee was doing it on purpose to get me to admit my feelings to Bree, but she wasn't even a part of the decision making process. It was actually Elyssa, who was arguably the least aware of my feelings for Bree since she hadn't been around for the first half of the trip, who insisted that Bree and I share a room.

"Why?" I asked. "I don't mind sharing the three-person room if that's the issue."

"No, you two take the two-person room," Elyssa said. "You're both tired and will want to go to sleep earlier than us, anyway."

That was an unfortunate part of me sharing a room with Elyssa — we always had wildly different sleep schedules. It had been an issue the year before as well since we were roommates in residence but we had managed well enough.

"I'm used to you staying up later than me," I said.

"Just take the room so we can all move on with our lives," Kiara said, rolling her eyes. "I want to go shower."

I sighed and took the key from Elyssa's hand.

"Okay," I said. "Goodnight, guys."

We'd already stopped for dinner and it was already starting to get dark out, so I didn't think we would be seeing each other again that night. I, for one, was ready to relax.

The room, as always, had one double bed in the middle. I went to the far side and threw my bag on the ground, and Bree did the same on the other side.

"Mind if I shower first?" She asked.

"I already showered this morning," I said.

"Perfect." She grabbed her toiletries and went into the bathroom. Meanwhile, I fell back on the bed and sighed deeply. Now that we had been to Algonquin and finished almost everything on my list, there wasn't much left on the trip to look forward to. We had to retrace our drive to get back to Elyssa's hometown to drop her off, then we were just going to be driving home. Granted, we were taking a different route, both to change things up a little and to avoid the towns where we'd royally embarrassed ourselves, but overall, it wasn't looking like the rest of the trip would be great. I suppose that was just an unfortunate part of road trips — at some point, you had to turn around and go home.

I got changed into my pyjamas then just sat around for a few minutes while I waited for Bree to get out of the shower. When she did, I grabbed my toiletries and went into the bathroom. It only took me a few minutes to finish brushing my teeth and washing my face. I walked back out again, only to run into Bree, who was stretching in the small area between the end of the bed and the bathroom door.

"Oh, um, sorry," I said. I took a step back so I wasn't in her personal space and my back hit the wall. I awkwardly shuffled sideways until I could walk around her then went to my side of the room, blushing fiercely.

"Sorry," she said with a sheepish grin. "It's the only part of the room that has enough space."

"It's no problem," I said. "Just took me by surprise."

She nodded and went back to stretching. Not wanting to make her uncomfortable, I sat down on the bed and diverted my attention. I grabbed my book out of my bag, one of the ones I'd bought at the bookstore near Kiara's house, and began reading.

A few minutes later, Bree stood back up and sat down on the other side of the bed. The mattress dipped slightly. I tried to focus on the words on the page, but I found my eyes drifting toward her more frequently than I would like to admit.

"Sorry you have to share a bed with me again," Bree said.

"What?" I asked in surprise. "I don't mind."

"I figured you didn't, but you argued against it pretty hard."

"I just felt bad making the three of them share," I

lied. "Since Kiara and Harlee shared the three-person room last night, and I was in the two-person."

Bree nodded, a twinkle in her eye. "Sure. That's what it was."

"I don't know what you're talking about," I said. I put my book and phone down on the nightstand to indicate that I was ready to go to sleep (and therefore let this conversation go before it led to something that I didn't want).

"Think we'll end up cuddling in our sleep again?" Bree asked, with a sly look in my direction.

I paused and stared back at her. "Would that be so bad?"

It was like we were in the cottage again, the way we were staring at each other. It was obvious that we both had the same thing on our minds. The only difference was that this time, I kissed her.

The sparks flew between us again. There was no denying that Bree and I had chemistry. She leaned further into the kiss, pushing me back against the headboard. As someone who was always the top in previous relationships, the power dynamic of both the first time we hooked up and this time felt unusual to me, but I tried to lean into it. I would let Bree do anything.

She swung her leg over mine so she was straddling me and I moaned with pleasure at the mere closeness. Her hands brushed against my stomach, making my nightdress ride up until I eventually pulled it over my head. She did the same with her shirt. Unlike me, she wasn't wearing a bra, and I choked a little at the sight of her. Of course, I'd seen her naked when we went skinny-dipping but this was on an entirely different level.

"Having second thoughts?" She asked with a grin. The logical part of my brain was screaming *yes! Stop this before it's too late!* But the rest of me wanted to just do this now and worry about the consequences later.

"Never," I responded. She began kissing me again. Her fingers ran through my hair, finally settling at the base of my neck. Her lips were soft, her breath minty and fresh, and I didn't know how I'd gone so long not touching her like this.

She kissed along my jawline and neck. Her soft lips tickled my sensitive skin. She paused in her movements when she reached my collarbone, then began licking and sucking on the skin. I pressed my body forward against her, wanting more, wanting *her.* She sucked on my skin until I was sure that it would leave a mark, then pulled back and stared at me. My heart was pounding in my chest, and I was very wet. If she didn't do something to me soon, I would probably start grinding on her leg.

"Sit on my face," she ordered. She didn't have to tell me twice. She rolled onto her back and I positioned myself on top of her, balancing myself with a hand on the headboard. It was a good thing I did, too, because the second her tongue hit my clit, I almost fell over from pleasure.

It was perfect. If I'd thought the last time was perfect then I was sorely mistaken, because this was on an entirely different level.

When we were done, I more or less fell back down on the bed. Bree moved so she was lying on top of me, with her forearms resting on either side of my head, her legs straddling me. Our bodies were pressed against each other, her soft skin brushing mine. I was gasping for breath, still reeling from what just happened, as we just stared at each other intently. And before I could consider the implications of what I was saying, before I'd even really thought it, I said, "I'm in love with you."

32

BREE WAS STILL asleep and half on top of me in the morning, which turned out to be very inconvenient since I was woken up by a persistent knocking at the door. As gently as I could, I slipped out from under her and stood up. I was about to answer the door when I realized that I was dressed only in a bra and some boxers that I had slid on just before falling asleep, which was hardly appropriate attire. The knocking on the door was getting louder by the second, so in a panic, I grabbed a towel and wrapped it around me like I'd just gotten out of the shower. It wasn't perfect but it was better than nothing.

I glanced out the peephole of the door and sighed in relief when I noticed it was just Harlee, and not some motel worker telling us we had slept through our checkout time or something. I swung open the door.

"Hey," I said. I thought I sounded pretty casual but I guess I didn't do a very good job because she narrowed her eyes immediately.

"Hey," she said suspiciously, looking me up and down.

"What's up?" I asked.

"Why are you wearing a bra and a towel?" She asked. "And looking like you haven't even taken a shower yet?"

I thought fast on my feet. "I was about to get in the shower when I heard you knocking. Sorry, did we oversleep?"

She glanced at the time on her phone and shrugged.

"No, it's not very late," she said. "But we were thinking of going to the diner down the street for breakfast. Do you want to join?"

"Um..." I glanced behind me. Bree was still fast asleep. Even if I woke her up right then, it would be a while before she was awake enough to go, and I didn't want her to wake up alone. I turned back to Harlee. "No, I don't think we'll be ready soon enough."

"Do you want us to bring you something back?"

"Sure, could you bring me some French toast, and get Bree pancakes with extra whipped cream and strawberries on top?"

Harlee smirked. It took me a moment to realize that it was probably because I didn't even try to hide the fact that I knew her breakfast order off by heart — but that didn't mean anything, did it? Friends knew each other's orders all the time, and there wasn't anything strange about it.

"Of course," Harlee said. "We'll be back within the hour."

I nodded. "Sounds good."

I closed the door again. I considered waking Bree up but I figured I should let her rest as long as possible — and, of course, I wanted to put off the conversation I knew we would inevitably need to have about everything that happened the night before.

After I'd professed my love, Bree hadn't really said anything. I think we were both a little out of it. We both just pretended that nothing had happened and went to sleep. There was every possibility that she would continue to pretend nothing happened between us, which would probably be the ideal situation until we got home from the road trip, but that wasn't really her style. She didn't like to leave things unsaid.

I took a longer shower than usual that morning, thinking over everything. I told myself what happened the night before hadn't been a big deal, just like the last time. By the time I got out of the shower, I almost believed it.

I finished getting ready and walked into the main room again. By that point, Bree was awake and dressed. We exchanged a quick 'hello' before she went to brush her teeth. Nothing out of the usual there, except for the absurd amount of tension in the air.

We didn't get a chance to speak alone again all day. By the time Bree got out of the bathroom, Kiara was in our room with the food they'd gotten us from the diner. Then, we got in the car and headed out.

We didn't have anywhere we really wanted to stop that day either, and it was a little too chilly to be able to comfortably spend time outside on a picnic or some-thing, so we decided to get a lot of the drive done that day. Although we'd scheduled three weeks out for the road trip, it was probably ideal for everyone if we got home early. For Kiara and Harlee's sake, it meant that they had more time to relax before they had to start work. For Elyssa, it gave her more time at her mom's place, before she switched to her dad's place at the end of the month. For Bree and me, it meant we didn't have to sit in this uncomfortable silence for much longer.

There was a moment during the car ride where it seemed like Harlee, Kiara, and Elyssa were all asleep, and Bree and I were awake. I considered having the conversation then, but I felt a little strange doing so, full well knowing the other three could wake up at any time, so I stayed quiet. Unfortunately, that meant also being stuck with my thoughts.

I continued to try to tell myself that it was no big deal. So I said I was in love with Bree — people said weird stuff after having sex. It didn't mean anything. At the very least, she didn't know that it meant anything, regardless of my feelings. But the tension between us was strong enough that it had me questioning my thoughts. Why wasn't Bree speaking to me? Was she normally this quiet or was this something new? Did I cross a line with what I said? What if I ruined our friendship, just like I'd been worried about?

When we got to the motel, I went to check us in. When I got back, Kiara said, "You, me, and Harlee are sharing a room tonight."

"Okay," I said. I handed Elyssa the key to the other room and watched her walk off with Bree. There went any chance I had of being able to talk to Bree alone tonight.

Oh well, I thought. *Maybe it's for the best. More time to think this over.*

As always, Harlee and Kiara shared one bed, and I took the other. It was a good thing that I had the bed to myself because I was up tossing and turning for ages. I never should have said it. I was just so caught up in the moment that I let my emotions take over for a moment without any filter. Obviously, Bree did not reciprocate my feelings; if she did, she would have said something, or at least indicated it, by now.

There was only one thing I could do. I had to take it all back, and hope that she was willing to forget it.

🦋 33 🦋

OUR DRIVE FOR THE NEXT DAY was set up to be another boring one since we didn't have anything planned for the return trip home, so when Kiara screamed about seeing a waterfall, I didn't mind pulling over.

The waterfall was in a park so I had to turn off the road and drive down a long path to get to it. Finally, we reached a small dirt parking lot and all jumped out.

"Come on!" Kiara yelled. She ran off toward the waterfall and Harlee followed quickly after her. Elyssa went a little more slowly.

Bree paused by the wooden fence that separated the forested area from the parking lot and knelt down to tie her shoe. My stomach leapt into my throat. This was my chance. It was a little more public than I wanted it to be for the conversation we were going to have, but I didn't know the next time I would get to speak to Bree alone.

She stood up again and began to walk toward the waterfall. I put my arm out to stop her, and she jumped in surprise. She probably hadn't noticed that I was still there too.

"Can I talk to you for a second, Bree?" I asked.

She nodded. "Of course."

We moved off to the side and I looked behind her to make sure the other three were far enough away that they wouldn't hear what we were saying.

"Is everything all right?" Bree asked. I hesitated. Did she really not know what I was going to say?

"I thought we should talk about the other night," I said. I subtly rubbed my sweaty hands on my pants. I wasn't usually one to get nervous, but what I was about to say had me freaking out. "About... what I said."

"Oh," Bree said. "Right."

Her face didn't give away how she felt about the situation at all which I found a little disconcerting.

"Right," I echoed. I found myself at a loss for words. "Um... I just wanted you to know that I didn't..." I cleared my throat. "I didn't mean what I said the other night. I was just caught up in the moment. I'm not in love with you."

The typical small smile that had been on her face slowly slid off. I didn't understand why. I thought she would be relieved to know that I hadn't meant it, that everything could go back to normal once we got home from the trip.

"I hope this doesn't change anything between us," I continued when she didn't say anything. "I know we said that last time and then it happened again, but I really mean it. I don't want to complicate our feelings or anything."

Bree stayed silent. I only got more worried as the

time passed. Shouldn't she be saying that that's how she feels too and that of course, we can go back to normal? I looked around awkwardly as I waited, unable to stare at her face any longer.

Finally, she took in a breath like she was going to say something. I looked at her. She paused.

"I don't want to be your fuck buddy, April," she said in a cold voice. My mouth dropped in shock. Is that really what she thought I was asking of her? "So if that's what you're looking for, find someone else."

My mouth went dry. This wasn't the response I expected, and I hadn't planned anything to say to it. In fact, I couldn't think of anything to say to it because I was too busy trying to figure out why she said it, especially in that tone. Was it possible that she thought I'd been serious before, and felt special that I loved her, even if she didn't feel the same way? Or was it possible that she secretly *did* feel the same way, and that was why she was being so cold about it? What if she thought I was pulling her aside to say it again, and she was going to say it back?

Or was I just projecting what I wanted the situation to be?

I wanted to take back what I said and tell her that I'd just lied because I was scared of her reaction. I wanted to tell her that I didn't just see her as a fuck buddy or friend with benefits, but as someone that I'd slowly been developing feelings for over the past couple of weeks. But I didn't want to stick my neck out like that when I couldn't know how she would react or respond.

I guess I was stuck in my thoughts for a little too long because before I even opened my mouth, before I even knew what to say, Bree stormed off. I slammed my head against the wooden pole next to me and wondered how I kept making everything worse.

⚜

In my room that night, I pulled out the list and a pencil. There was a mistake I needed to fix.

I laid out the list on the nightstand and scrubbed at the small checkmark with the small pink eraser. The pencil was cheap so the eraser was pretty crap. I nearly ripped the paper as I rubbed at it. But finally, the check-mark faded from the page.

Fall in love — real love. It hadn't happened with Tina, and I'd ruined any chance I had at that happening with Bree.

34

I MIGHT HAVE BEEN IMAGINING IT, but I thought the tension could be felt in the air. It was raining again outside — honestly, wasn't it supposed to rain in April then be nice in May? — so we were all piled into Harlee, Kiara, and Bree's room since it had more space. I'd assumed we would all talk or do something when we got inside but we were sitting in total silence.

The clock on the nightstand ticked with every passing second. Harlee's book page scraped against another as she turned it. Every time Kiara chewed down on her gum, it made an awful squishing noise that made me squirm. Elyssa was humming under her breath. The rain was hitting the window loudly, and Bree was staring at it. Nobody said a word.

I just sat there and stewed in the fact that it was all my fault.

When we were camping, I'd told Bree that the trip was even better than I'd imagined it. And that was true to an extent — we'd had some really great times in the past couple of weeks. But if there was one thing I regretted about the trip, it was the level of tension I had caused the entire time. Even before Bree and I hooked up at the cottage, I'd been so worried about what I might do around her that everyone else even noticed. Then, after the cottage, both of us had been so awkward around each other that it was having a noticeable effect on the group. I felt really bad about that.

"Hey, I know something we need to do!" Kiara said. We all looked at her. "We need to finish the 'thirty things to do before thirty' list!"

"Oh yeah, I forgot we still haven't done that," Elyssa said. "That's the last thing on the list, right?"

Honestly, with everything else that had been going on in my life, I'd completely forgotten about the list as well. I grabbed it from my bag and looked over it quickly. I faltered when I passed fall in love, with the remnants of the erased checkmark next to it. Nobody else could see the list, though, so I didn't need to explain why that wasn't there.

"Yeah, it's the last thing," I said. If it hadn't been for *fall in love*, it wouldn't have been a lie.

"Awesome!" Kiara said. She pulled out a notebook and a pen. "This won't take any time at all!"

I found that a little doubtful given how long it took me to come up with the list in high school, but I didn't want to ruin her optimism.

"There's five of us, so each of us just needs to come up with six things to do," Harlee said. "That's pretty easy."

"Let's each write out six things and then we'll share

them in a few minutes," Kiara suggested. "Then I'll write them on the official list."

That seemed like a good enough plan to me. I wasn't sure why she wanted to write the list instead of me but I didn't care so long as I would be able to stop her from writing anything too terrible down, even if someone suggested it. I opened my notes app. I'd already brainstormed a little before this, so I already had a few items written down. They probably weren't the best ideas in the world, but I was sure the other suggestions would be pretty stupid too so I decided to just use them.

"Okay, I'm done!" Kiara said triumphantly a few minutes later, dropping her pen. "How about everyone else?"

"I'm ready," I said.

"Me too," Harlee said.

"Same," Elyssa said. Bree nodded.

"I'll go first," Kiara said. "I took a lot of inspiration from the current list, I'm not going to lie. So, learn a third language, get another tattoo, run another race to prove the first one wasn't a fluke--"

"Hey!"

"Shush, I'm reading. Anyway, where was I? Oh right, learn to bartend, travel alone, and go to a concert." She smiled at me.

"That sounds good," I said.

"You just copied the current list," Bree said. That was the first time I'd heard her speak that day, and it caused butterflies in my stomach. I tried to focus on the paper in front of Kiara and pretend it hadn't happened.

"It's better than nothing!" Kiara said. "Who wants to go next? Harlee?"

"Sure. I went the more practical route," Harlee said. She cleared her throat and read off her phone. "Get a full-time job that pays well, start saving for retirement, pay off any student loans, learn first-aid, learn self-defence, and go vegan."

"Go vegan?" Kiara asked.

"She mentioned last year that it was one of her life goals," Harlee said. "Might as well try to do it in the next ten years."

Kiara still looked a little confused but she wrote it down. The thought of having to do all this in the next ten years was a little overwhelming to me, and I wondered whether I was going to put off a lot of the list until the last minute like I did this time.

"I'll go next," Elyssa said in a soft tone. "Adopt a pet, visit every province in Canada, go wine-tasting, start a vegetable garden, go sky diving, and of course, make a 'forty things to do before forty' list."

"That last one is cheating!" Kiara said, with an accusing finger pointed in Elyssa's direction.

"Somebody had to say it," Elyssa said calmly.

"It was a given," Kiara said. She wrote all of them down. "All right, Bree, you're up!"

"Okay." She shifted forward in her chair. I found myself leaning in, excited to hear what she had written for me. I wondered if she was going to suggest something terrible because she was mad at me but I quickly brushed those thoughts aside. Bree wasn't like that. "Um, I did my best to write things April has told me she wants to do. So, first, go see a broadway show, learn how to ride a motorcycle, learn sign language, which goes with learn a third language

I guess, go backpacking, try freediving, and buy a house."

All of those were things I'd mentioned to her in late-night chats we'd had back in residence. I was surprised she'd remembered them all, but I suppose I shouldn't have been. I tried to make eye contact with Bree but she was looking at her phone still.

Thank you, I thought. *Thank you for caring enough to remember my dreams.*

Kiara nodded as she wrote.

"Perfect!" She said. She looked at me. "All right April, we just need yours."

Everything I wrote suddenly seemed so boring compared to what they said, but I couldn't be the one person not to contribute, especially considering it was for my own bucket list.

"Right," I said. I opened the notes app on my phone again. "Okay, um, live abroad, have an outrageous birthday party, fall in love—"

"You already had fall in love on this list," Elyssa interrupted. She pointed at the paper, her finger covering up where the checkmark used to be. Thank goodness she hadn't noticed. "Number eleven, remember?"

But I didn't.

"I meant fall in love again," I said. "Since I'm not with that girl anymore. Sorry, I should have clarified."

I watched as Kiara wrote (again) on the list, the guilt eating at my heart.

"What else, what else?" Kiara asked eagerly.

"Oh, right. Write a letter to open in ten years, see the seven natural wonders of the world, and..." there was a lump in my throat as I stared at #6.

"And?" Kiara prompted.

I struggled to say it. "And reconnect with Tina."

"Tina?" Kiara asked. Her eyebrows knit together.

"My ex-girlfriend," I said. It was probably a vain hope but I wanted to see if I could fix things.

"Oh." An awkward silence hung in the air as she wrote it down. "And that's it! The 'thirty things to do before you're thirty list is complete!"

I smiled. "Great!"

Elyssa slid a pen toward me.

"Want to make it official?" She asked, looking at the current list that was lying in front of me. I stared at the page. I'd done it. I couldn't believe I'd actually fulfilled this dream. I took the pen from Elyssa's hand and officially checked it off.

Kiara, Harlee, and Elyssa cheered.

"You're done!" Kiara exclaimed. Harlee put on some music to celebrate. Their excitement was infectious, and I soon found myself dancing and laughing along.

Instinctively, I looked over at Bree. We made eye contact for one second — one second that felt like an eternity. Then she snapped her head away and stared at the wall, which was like a knife in my chest.

In the midst of all the celebrations around me, the smile sank from my face as I realized that Bree wanted nothing to do with me.

35

THE NEXT NIGHT was Elyssa's last night with us on the trip. We had mapped out the return trip well enough that we knew we were dropping her off at her house the next day. As such, we were going out to a bar as a sort of goodbye. Unfortunately, unlike all my friends, I wasn't really in the mood.

I hoped I would feel more like it once I was ready to go, so I got ready with the rest of them, but still, all I could think about was Bree and the look on her face when I said I didn't love her.

As my friends all argued over which bar to go to and Kiara ordered an Uber, I sank to a seat on the end of the bed.

"Hey, I don't really feel like going out tonight, guys," I said in a small voice. "Sorry."

They all stopped talking and looked at me. I felt really bad bailing on Elyssa on her final night, but I didn't think I would be much fun to be around anyway.

"Do you want us to stay back with you?" Elyssa asked in concern.

Kiara frowned. "The Uber will be here in a minute. Should I cancel?"

I shook my head and forced a smile.

"That's okay," I said. "You guys go have fun."

She didn't look entirely convinced. I didn't know how to say that I didn't want to be around anyone at that moment really, least of all Bree. I needed some time to work through my feelings on my own.

"You know what, I think I want to stay back too," Harlee said. I frowned. She had been the most excited to go out, which meant she was definitely only staying back for my benefit. "I'm a little tired."

"Oh, okay," Elyssa said. She looked a little disappointed, but also relieved that she wouldn't be leaving me alone. "I guess we'll see you guys later, then."

"Have fun!" Harlee said. Elyssa, Kiara, and Bree walked outside. Harlee sat down on the other bed and faced me.

"You didn't need to stay back with me," I said. "I would be fine on my own."

Harlee waved dismissively and pulled out her phone.

"I don't mind," she said. "Now what do you want from UberEats? Pizza?"

"I— what?" The conversation had done a total one-eighty and I was a little confused.

"You're upset," she said simply. "And whenever any of us is upset, we order comfort food. So what do you want?"

"Pizza works," I said. I wasn't in the mood for anything in particular, but Harlee wouldn't have taken that for an answer. She nodded and quickly typed something in on her phone. Once the order was in, she threw her phone to the side and looked at me.

"So," she said, "obviously something happened."

"A couple of somethings," I muttered. I took a deep breath. "Um, Bree and I slept together again, I told her I was in love with her, then took it back, and now she won't talk to me."

Harlee nodded, though her face was one of pure shock.

"Sorry, this all happened in the past five days?" She asked.

I nodded. I couldn't blame her for being surprised; it was a lot.

"Okay..." Harlee said slowly. "Well... Bree's probably just a little upset right now and needs some time to deal with everything that happened. I'm sure she'll come around."

"No," I said. I shook my head and blinked back my tears. "No, I confessed my feelings and it ruined everything, just like I thought it would!"

"Why did you take them back?" Harlee questioned. "If those were your real feelings, why would you tell her they weren't?"

I shrugged, my hands shaking. "I thought it would fix it. I thought she would see that it was all just one big mistake and I didn't mean any of it."

Harlee moved from her spot and sank down beside me on the bed.

"Are you in love with her?" She asked seriously.

To my utter shock and dismay, I was unable to hold back the tears that had been threatening to spill over. I thought it was only a couple coming down so I quickly wiped them away, but they began coming down faster and faster until I was fully sobbing. Poor Harlee was completely out of her element. She patted me on the shoulder lightly, but if anything, that only made me more uncomfortable and upset.

"Yes," I cried. Harlee's hand froze. "I'm in love with her and now I ruined everything. I never should have said anything!"

Her hand began moving again, though this time it was notably slower, like she was lost in thought as she did it.

"It will be okay," she said. Her voice wasn't as convincing as I think she meant for it to be.

"No." I shook my head. My vision, already blurry from the tears, completely disappeared for a few moments. "No, I'll never be able to fix this. Bree hates me!"

Harlee didn't have anything to say to that, because really, what was there to say?

✤ 36 ✤

BREE WAS DRIVING SLOWER than usual the next day. At first, I was confused, but I surmised quickly that she wanted the drive to Elyssa's house to last as long as possible because we were saying goodbye to her there.

Ideally, we would have stayed at her place for a few days again, but we were getting close to the three-week mark, and we were all itching to get home. It was probably for the best in the long run anyway; who knows what crazy shit Bree and I might have gotten into at the cottage this time around.

I wanted to talk to Elyssa, maybe ask her about her plans for the rest of the summer, but there was a tense silence in the car that I didn't want to break. So instead of talking to her, I looked out the window and cringed at the memory of crying in front of Harlee the night before.

The landscape began to look familiar to me as we pulled onto Elyssa's long street. Bree drove with practiced ease as if she had done this drive a million times, rather than just once before. She pulled into Elyssa's driveway and parked the car. Nobody moved for a few moments.

"Thanks for inviting me on the trip guys," Elyssa said finally. "I had a lot of fun."

She opened her door and climbed out. The rest of us got out after her to say goodbye.

"It was nice to see you again, Elyssa," Bree said. She hugged her. "Thanks for coming along."

I went next. I hugged her tightly, maybe even tighter than I had when we moved out of residence. It was painful to only get to see her for a few days, then have to say goodbye all over again.

"I'll see you in September," I said. She nodded and pulled back, then held her hand up for a high five. I obliged.

"Roommates," she said.

"I can't wait," I responded.

I stepped back so the others could say goodbye. Kiara and Harlee stepped forward together. While they did that, Bree and I stood by the front of the car in frigid silence.

When it became too much for me, I said, "I can take over driving now, if you want."

Bree didn't even spare me a glance.

"It's fine," she said. "I know you hate driving in the country with no directions. We can switch at the gas station by the highway."

Despite her tone, it made me feel nice that she cared enough to think of that.

"Okay," I said. "Thanks."

She nodded ever so slightly.

"Hey, April, do you mind helping me carry my other bag in?" Elyssa asked. She nodded toward the duffel bag on the ground right next to me.

"Oh yeah, of course." I picked it up and walked with her to the house.

"You can just leave it there," she said once we were in the mudroom. "I'll come to get it after."

"Okay."

I went to go back outside, figuring she would follow me, but she put her hand on my shoulder to stop me. I looked back.

"Is everything all right?" I asked. She wrung her hands nervously.

"Looks, I know it's not my place to intervene with any of this," she said, "but I just want you to know that Bree is really unhappy with the way things are between you two right now."

I sighed. "Elyssa—"

"I'm not telling you what to do," she interrupted quickly. "What's going on is between you and Bree. I just... I don't want to see you throw away a good thing."

Was this her way of telling me that Bree liked me too? Was she telling me to go after it?

My thoughts swirling, I just nodded. She nodded too and we walked back out to the driveway. I barely paid attention as we said our final goodbyes and got back in the car, too caught up in thinking about Bree.

Neither of us were happy with the situation. I was still hopelessly in love with her but she didn't know. As far as I knew, she thought I wanted to just sleep with her, no strings attached. There was definitely a message that got twisted somewhere in there, and it was my fault.

I looked at Bree in the driver's seat. Her hair was thrown up in a messy bun on top of her head — one of the only times I'd seen her choose not to style it. Her face was tight from concentration. Her knuckles were white because of her grip on the steering wheel. Outside of exam season, I had never seen her this stressed and I felt immensely guilty.

Don't throw away a good thing.

❦ 37 ❦

THAT NIGHT, I had a dream that I made up with Bree. In the dream, we weren't on the road trip anymore. We were back in her room at residence, and I had just returned from meeting up with Tina. The conversation had gone as well as I could have liked; we mutually agreed that the way we ended things was not ideal and we should have talked things through sooner instead of pulling away for so long that there seemed to be no chance of repairing it. We talked about how we should have put the friendship before the relationship, should have agreed in the first place that we would go back to being friends, even if we didn't work out as girlfriends. She reminded me that sometimes things don't work out and that's okay.

After that talk, I went to Bree's room to talk about it. When we lived in residence, Bree was the only one of us with a single room — I shared a room with Elyssa, and Kiara shared a room with Harlee. We would spend most of our time in Kiara and Harlee's room, but sometimes when I just needed a friend, I went to Bree alone. Similar to real life, in the dream, we were on really bad terms, but she let me inside anyway because she's just like that. Even when she's mad at you, she's the sweetest person on earth. I sat on her bed, which was set to the highest level, and hugged her penguin squishmallow like I always did when I was upset (of course, if she ever told anyone about that, I would deny it). At first, I only told her about what just happened with Tina, but the conversation quickly changed to be about us.

Eventually, I told her that I hadn't been lying when I said I was in love with her, and that I wanted a proper relationship but had been too scared to say so. She stared at me for a few minutes, then began laughing. Really laughing, to the point that tears streamed down her face. I was really confused and didn't understand why, until she managed to choke out that she was in love with me too.

Then I woke up and was disappointed to find out it hadn't really happened.

Of course, the dream was very unrealistic for a number of reasons. First of all, we'd moved out of residence a month before and we would never live in those rooms again. Second, I had talked to Tina, which I was pretty sure I was never going to do again in real life, no matter what I'd written on that list. And third, Bree said she was in love with me too.

The dream did help me in one way, though. That "conversation" with Tina showed me where I'd gone wrong in everything with Bree — I'd been so worried about ruining my friendship by confessing my feelings that I'd ruined my friendship by not telling her the truth.

Unfortunately, I wasn't sure whether telling her how I really felt now would make any difference after all the harm I caused.

38

THE DRIVES WERE GETTING LONG and tedious. We were all tired. We all just wanted to get home. While I definitely didn't regret the trip, I wished we'd planned a little bit better, so we wouldn't be too burned out to enjoy it by the end.

We stopped at an ON route because Kiara and I were hungry. Bree and Harlee stayed in the car. We went inside and ordered, then moved to the side to wait. I considered making conversation but I didn't really feel like it, and it didn't look like Kiara did either.

The back wall of the ON route was glass. I stood near it with my hands in my hoodie pocket. To pass the time as I waited for my food, I looked out the window. Bree and Harlee were standing next to the car now. They were talking about something, but I couldn't understand what from this far away. Bree's hands were waving wildly. The wind was blowing her long ponytail all over the place. When she smiled, her eyes crinkled a little. I'd missed her smile the past few days.

I wanted to go out there and kiss her. I wanted to tell her how I felt, how I'd lied before because I didn't want to ruin everything. I wanted to hold her and never let go.

Stop it, April, I told myself. But I didn't stop staring. I didn't stop imagining. After all, things were so bad between us that I didn't see how I could possibly make it any worse.

My feet were moving of their own volition. I was walking out the door. Kiara called after me, probably asking why I was leaving without my food, but I didn't respond.

Harlee and Bree hadn't noticed me yet. When I was only a few feet away, I called out, "Bree!" She turned towards me. I quickly closed the distance between us, pulled her close, and kissed her like it was our last night on earth.

"What was that?" Bree asked when we pulled away. Her eyes were wide with surprise.

"I lied," I whispered. I rested my forehead against hers. "I do want you. I do love you."

Bree smiled widely. Then she kissed me back.

39

"WHY DID YOU say it wasn't true?" Bree asked. We were sitting on the bed we were sharing that night. After we dropped off Elyssa, we planned to go back to sharing one room with two beds again, but given everything that had happened that day, we all thought it was best for Bree and I to get our own room to talk some things out.

"I thought that it would be worse if I told you the truth," I said. "That it would ruin everything between us. I'm sorry. I shouldn't have lied to you."

She looked down at her hands. She twisted the ring around her middle finger nervously.

"No, it's fine," she said. "I get it. In a way, I guess I did the same."

"What?" I asked. "What do you mean?"

"I almost said something," she said. "That night, when you first said it to me. But I chickened out at the last second because I was worried that you hadn't actually meant it."

"And then I told you I didn't."

She nodded, chewing on her lower lip. It had been a nervous habit of hers for as long as I knew her. I grabbed her hand and rubbed my thumb over the back of it, just wanting to make her feel better however I could. She smiled at me.

"We called it," she said.

I tilted my head. "What do you mean?"

"We always said we'd end up together one day," she said. With her spare hand, she tucked my hair behind my ear. Then she kissed me again and I knew everything was going to turn out fine after all.

❧

The next morning, I woke up earlier than Bree. Outside, the sun was shining and the birds were chirping. All I wanted to do was go for a swim in the pool before we left, so I got out of bed immediately to get ready. Bree had been hugging me in her sleep, so she groaned a little as I pulled away but she didn't wake up.

As I went to grab my clothes, my hand brushed against the piece of paper safely tucked against the side of the bag. The bucket list.

Now that we had worked things out, I felt like I could properly enjoy the celebration of finishing the whole list. Well, almost the whole list.

I smiled back at Bree, who looked angelic lying there. Then I pulled out a pencil and checked off *fall in love — real love*. Sometimes, you just know.

❧ 40 ❧

OUR LAST DAY of the trip was a warm one, so we drove with the windows down, the sunroof open, and the music blasting. Contrary to how most of us had felt for the past few days, we were all very energetic and singing along to the song at the top of our lungs.

Once we passed the WELCOME TO EAST PORT sign, I turned down the music a little.

"Hey, where should I drop you guys?" I asked, turning my head slightly toward the backseat. "Harlee's house?"

"Yeah, that's probably easiest," Kiara said. I nodded. A minute later, I was pulling into her driveway.

Unlike when we said goodbye to Elyssa, Bree and I didn't get out to hug them goodbye. Harlee wasn't huge on hugs anyway, and Kiara had a thing about not hugging goodbye — she said it made hugs feel sad.

"Thanks for doing this, guys," Kiara said. "I had a lot of fun."

I smiled and nodded — I was running out of ways to

tell people I also had fun on the road trip. Bree leaned over me so she could talk out the window.

"Hey, good luck dealing with your parents, Kiara," she said. I laughed. I'd totally forgotten about that whole situation.

Kiara grimaced. "Thanks, I'm going to need it."

"Remember, two weeks until you leave for camp," Harlee said. Kiara perked up at the mention of her summer job.

"I hope being at camp will be as exciting as this trip," she said.

"Are you excited to start work, Harlee?" Bree asked.

Harlee shrugged. "Yeah, I guess. It will give me something to do. But I doubt I'll have a very interesting summer."

I got the sense that wouldn't be the case, but I was pretty sure Harlee wanted a more relaxed summer and I didn't want to burst her bubble.

"Well, if we don't see you before then, good luck with your jobs!" I said. My hope was that I would be able to meet up with them again during the summer, or at least Harlee since Kiara and Elyssa weren't exactly nearby, but it was hard to say whether or not that would work out when we all had summer jobs.

"You too!" Kiara said.

I didn't want to drag our goodbye out any longer, although I knew Bree and Kiara could talk for hours, so I pulled out of the driveway and waved at them one last time before driving off.

Bree slipped her hand in mine. I was going to have to get better at driving with only my left hand since we would be driving like this a lot.

"It's going to be a good summer," Bree said.

I looked at her for a moment. Her bright eyes, her rosy cheeks, the brilliant smile on her face. I couldn't believe how lucky I was to be with this girl.

"Yeah," I said. "It will be."

ABOUT THE AUTHOR

Isabel Hansen is an emerging Canadian author. She writes lesbian romance stories. *Scarlet Sun* is her debut novel. She can be found online at isabelhansen.com and on instagram @isabelhansen_author.